Artsy-Fartsy

AN ALDO ZELNICK COMIC NOVEL

Written by Karla Oceanak

Illustrated by Kendra Spanjer

BAILIWICK PRESS

Copyright © 2009 by Karla Oceanak and Kendra Spanjer

Published by:
Bailiwick Press
309 East Mulberry Street
Fort Collins, Colorado 80524
(970) 672-4878
Fax: (970) 672-4731
www.bailiwickpress.com
www.aldozelnick.com

Book design by:
Launie Parry
Red Letter Creative
red-letter-creative.com

Manufactured by:
Friesens Corporation, Altona, Canada
October 2010
Job # 59972

ISBN 978-1-934649-04-6

Library of Congress Control Number: 2009938889

18 17 16 15 14 13 12 11 10   7 6 5 4 3 2

Dear Aldo –
Here's a gift to start off
your summer vacation.
It's a sketchbook
for recording all your
artsy-fartsy ideas!
I'm so proud of you.
All my love,
Goosy

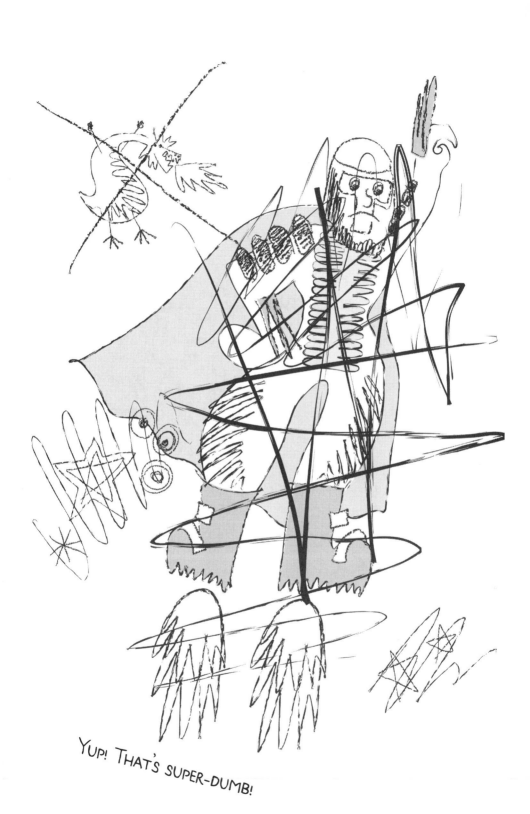

YUP! THAT'S SUPER-DUMB!

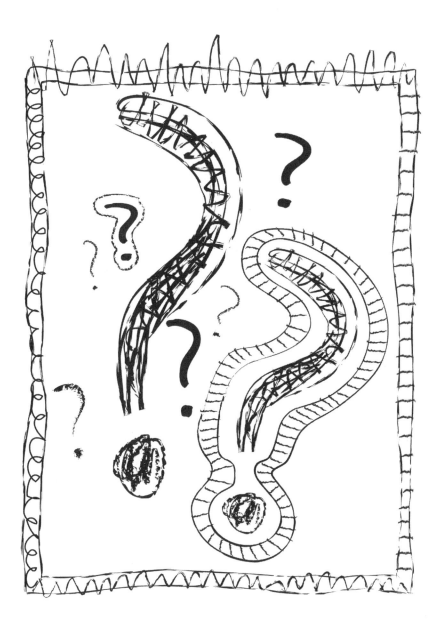

Umm...

So...

So Goosy gave me this sketchbook and said I should draw in it a little bit every day.

Goosy is my grandma. Her real name is Lucy. When I was little, I couldn't say Grandma Lucy, so I called her Goosy. Now everybody calls her that. I guess you'd say it's her nickname.

Goosy thinks I'm artistic just because I drew a few cute pictures when I was little.

NOT BAD!

GOOSY

CAT

YEAH RIGHT!

Also, one day when I was coloring, I put a pair of underwear on my head. Goosy thought it looked like I was wearing an artist's hat, so she took a picture of me.

(WHY did I put underwear on my head? I don't remember! I was only 3, for crying out loud!)

My family seems to think I'm going to take after Goosy, who is a painter. But that's totally absurd.*

On the other hand, I'm noticing that when people get ideas about you, those ideas tend to stick, like gum on the bottom of your shoe, or like nicknames.

*See the Word Gallery I made at the end of this sketchbook. It tells what the * words mean.

And I do kind of like to draw. I MIGHT even be good at it.

But the only other kids I know who draw are girls. Plus, last year my art teacher picked one of my drawings for the school bulletin board. It was... this is so embarrassing...a unicorn. And I made the mistake of calling it:

Tommy Geller, who lives in my neighborhood and goes to my school, gave ME a nickname then.

Sooooooooooo.....yeeaaaaaaaah. I'm not so sure it's good to be artsy-fartsy.*

And what am I supposed to draw in this sketchbook, anyway?

I don't KNOW what to draw!

I'm gonna go ask Mr. Mot. He's smart. He'll think of something cool.

I showed the sketchbook to Mr. Mot. He's our neighbor. He used to be an English teacher, but he's ancient* now.

MR. MOT
...IN 3,000 B.C.

He said, "Writers write about what they know, Aldo." (Some help he is. Sheesh.)

"Oh c'mon," I said. "I'm not supposed to write. I'm supposed to draw. This is a SKETCHbook..."

Mr. Mot is a word guy. He's all about words—special words, silly words, looooong words. I play checkers with him sometimes, and while we're playing, he likes to mix in his fancy words with the regular ones. I pretend I'm not listening, but later on, when I'm lying in my bed about to drift off to sleep, I whisper Mr. Mot's words to myself. They feel like rock candy in my mouth...clunky and complicated, but also sweet.

"It appears to me you are doing both," he pointed out as he looked over what I've already done. "An ambitious* amalgam*!"

"What?!"

"That means what you're doing is a challenging mixture. Not many people can write AND draw well."

"Amalgam, schmalgam!" I said. I was getting annoyed.* First Goosy tells me to draw, then Mr. Mot tells me to write. How's a kid on summer vacation supposed to get any relaxation time?

"OK, well now I don't know what to draw or write!" I frowned at him to emphasize my annoyedness.

"Perhaps," he said, "you should start at the very beginning. If you begin with A, you'll eventually end up at Z." Then he did something really crazy. He took the pencil he keeps tucked behind his ear and he put a tiny* mark by the interesting A words I'd written so far, like "artsy-fartsy" and "absurd." He winked at me and went back to reading his book.

Arg! What the heck is he talking about?

OK. So what's the very beginning?

Maybe...

THIS IS ME

My name is Aldo. It rhymes with Waldo...like the guy with the red striped shirt and funny hat in those *Where's Waldo?* books.

WHERE'S ALDO?

I was named after my great-grandfather Aldo. It's kind of a weird name, but I'm used to it.

Besides Goosy, the other people in my family are my mom, my dad, my brother, and Max.

15

DAD

MOM

GOOSY

TIMOTHY

MAX

Timothy is my big brother. He's 14. He's not home today because he's at baseball camp. He's a Super-Jock.

He's good at football. He's good at baseball. He's good at soccer. You get the idea. He's good at anything where you chase a ball around like a nitwit.

He's <u>athletic</u>.*

SEE WHAT I MEAN?

"GO OUTSIDE AND GET SOME EXERCISE, ALDO."

(MAN, HE MAKES ME LOOK BAD.)

I'm 10, and I'm NOT athletic. Sports aren't much fun, unless you're the sort of person who <u>enjoys</u> feeling sweaty and tired.

I enjoy things that involve sitting and lying down, preferably with pillows.

Which reminds me, it's the first day of summer vacation, and I haven't even watched any TV yet. See ya.

OUTSIDE

So I watched some TV.

Then my mom kicked me outside. Sheesh.

What's the problem with a kid watching a few cartoons?

"It's a beautiful day," Mom said. "Go do something OUTSIDE."

My mom has this thing about OUTSIDE. She always says it like that, like it's so important it has to be in capital letters. What's so great about OUTSIDE, anyway?

Trees, bugs, dog poop. Who cares? There's really nothing to do OUTSIDE.

BEE GARDEN
(I'M ALLERGIC.*)

FLAT BASKETBALL

ANTHILL
(KIND OF COOL)

YUP. I'M NOT
PLAYING HOPSCOTCH.

So I biked down the street to Jack's Dad-house and knocked on the door, but no one was home.

ARG! WHERE IS THAT GUY??

Jack is my best friend. We call this house his Dad-house because Jack's parents are divorced. Half the time he lives here, with his dad, and the rest of the time he lives around the corner in his Mom-house, with his mom and stepdad.

Next I went to Jack's Mom-house, but he wasn't there, either.

I ended up just hanging out here under this giant pine tree. It's at the edge of the park near my house.

MY DOG, MAX

X-RAY VIEW
(SEE THE DOTTED LINES?
YOU COULDN'T SEE ME OTHERWISE.)

This tree is a Colorado Blue Spruce. There are a lot of them here in Colorado. (Duh.)

It's dark and cool under this tree, and I can watch people walk by. They can't see me.

UH-OH, ABC GUM.* (NOT MINE.)

Hey, I could do whatever I wanted under this tree and no one would know...

Whoa! It's Jack.

How did he find me?

He is one alert* guy.

ROCK HOUND

Jack just got back from a trip with his dad to Nebraska. He was bringing his new Nebraska rocks to show me.

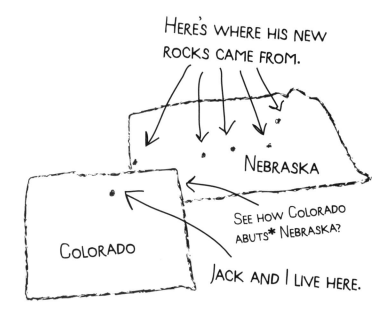

HERE'S WHERE HIS NEW ROCKS CAME FROM.

NEBRASKA

SEE HOW COLORADO ABUTS* NEBRASKA?

COLORADO

JACK AND I LIVE HERE.

Jack is a rock hound. That means he's crazy about collecting and identifying rocks. In his bedroom, he has shelves and shelves full of rocks, all labeled with where he found them and what kind they are.

I personally don't see how rocks are exciting. But the good thing is that all those rocks in his pockets slow Jack down. I'm one of the slowest runners at school, but when Jack and I race, I can almost keep up with him sometimes.

IF ONLY HE'D WEAR A BACKPACK FULL OF ROCKS TOO...

By the way, Jack liked it under the tree. He said we should turn it into a fort.

BAD NEWS

(ON THE OTHER HAND...
CHICKEN ENCHILADAS!)

I went home after my "bike ride," and Mom had made my favorite dinner.

I should have known that meant something was amiss.*

After we ate, my mom spilled the beans: She signed me up for summer baseball.

Only she didn't say it like it was bad news. She said it in her excited, happy voice: "Aldo, guess what? You get to start baseball tomorrow!"

I kind of threw a fit.

I yelled that I wouldn't do it. I begged Dad to get me out of it. (Usually I can count on Dad, but this time he took Mom's side.) I ran to my room and slammed the door.

HOW TO THROW A FIT

I'm just not going, that's all. What are they going to do...pick me up, glue a baseball glove to my hand, and carry me to the field?

I REFUSE TO PLAY BASEBALL!!!

THE FORT

This morning I tried to put the baseball episode behind me (since I'm not playing, anyway). Jack and I snuck a bag of pretzels and two sodas into my backpack and walked down to the secret spot under the giant pine tree.

First we swept aside all the pinecones and sticks. Then we ran back to my house to get an old couch cushion from the basement. We tucked the cushion up against the tree trunk so it would be like a fort futon, and we found a knot in the tree that holds two sodas perfectly.

WHAT THE HECK?

JUST KIDDING!

JACK'S DOG,
SLATE

After everything was set up, I sat down on the cushion, leaned back against the tree trunk, and laced my fingers behind my head. It was summer vacation, and Jack and I were living the good life.

"What would you do with a million dollars?" I asked Jack.

"Buy a million cool rocks."

31

"That's dumb."

Jack and I say "that's dumb" to each other all the time. But we only sort of mean it.

"OK, I'd buy half a million cool rocks and a doughnut shop," said Jack.

"Now you're talkin'," I said.

Jack reached into the backpack for the bag of pretzels and pulled out this sketchbook instead. I'd forgotten I'd put it there.

"That's mine," I said, reaching for it.

"What is it?"

"Goosy gave it to me. She wants me to try drawing this summer."

"That's dumb. Are you gonna?"

How do you tell your best friend that even though you're mostly cool, you just might be the tiniest bit artsy-fartsy?

"Maybe. If I show it to you, will you keep it a secret?"

"I'll keep it a secret until I sell it on eBay."

Jack's mom sells things on eBay. She always teases us about selling our stuff when we leave it lying around her house.

But the thing is, one day she might actually do it.

Jack was being a smart-aleck, but I could tell by the look on his face that he was cool with it. So I showed him the sketchbook. I flipped through

POP QUIZ: GUESS WHICH OF THESE THINGS
JACK'S MOM HASN'T SOLD ON EBAY?

ANSWER:
SHE'S SOLD ALL OF THEM ON EBAY, INCLUDING A CERAMIC FROG
AND A "VINTAGE TWINKIE," WHICH WENT FOR $84.75. WHO
WOULD PAY $84.75 FOR A TWINKIE YOU CAN'T EVEN EAT?!

it, and he stopped me at the drawing of him with his new Nebraska rocks.

"That's pretty good," he said. "But basalt is dark gray. That's the only thing you might want to change."

I'm going to put the sketchbook in the crook of this tree and come back to draw in it later. It feels like a nice addition to our fort.

SO, I PLAYED BASEBALL

Here's what happened:

1. Dad came home after work this afternoon, handed me a baseball uniform, and said he was ready to take me to baseball practice.

2. I said, "That's weird, because I'm not playing baseball."

3. Then Mom walked up and said that I needed EXERCISE. She said I couldn't play any video games, for the entire summer if I didn't play baseball.

DORKY SHIRT

DORKY STRIPED PANTS

4. I looked at Dad. He shrugged and said, "That's the deal, pal."

5. I put on the dorky uniform and went to baseball practice.

First we played catch, just to get warmed up. I got so warm that I beaned my coach in the head. After that, he seemed a little apprehensive.*

YOU'VE GOT QUITE AN ARM, KID.

Whenever I got near him, he'd hold up his baseball mitt to his face and talk to me through the little holes.

The throwing wasn't so bad, but then came the running. Coach made us practice running the bases. Austin was the first to go. He left home plate and took off in the wrong direction. Instead of going to first base, he ran to third.

Alex, the first base kid,
was yelling at Austin to stop.
But Austin was concentrating
on running fast and didn't notice.
So Alex got all apoplectic.*
That's what Mr. Mot calls
it when people get hopping
mad and red and frustrated.

WRONG WAY!
WRONG WAAAAAY!

As Austin rounded second
base and headed to first, Alex held out
his arms to get Austin to stop, but Austin
knocked him over and kept right on running.
(I think Austin might have baseball confused with
football.)

DUDE! THIS IS NOT A TACKLE SPORT!

To calm everyone down, Coach had us all get in a line behind him and follow him as he ran the bases. We ran the whole loop 10 times without stopping. It was abominable.*

COACH

—ME

Okay, so I only ran 8 loops because I got lapped (TWICE), but still. And it turned out that the fastest kid on the team is a GIRL. When she ran by me, I stuck out my tongue at her—just a little, so Coach couldn't tell if I was sticking out my tongue or just breathing hard.

Show-off. ⟶

I'M A GIRL AND I RUN FAST. NAH, NAH, NANANAH!

I'm putting the sketchbook back in the tree now because Jack and I are fortin' it up later tonight.

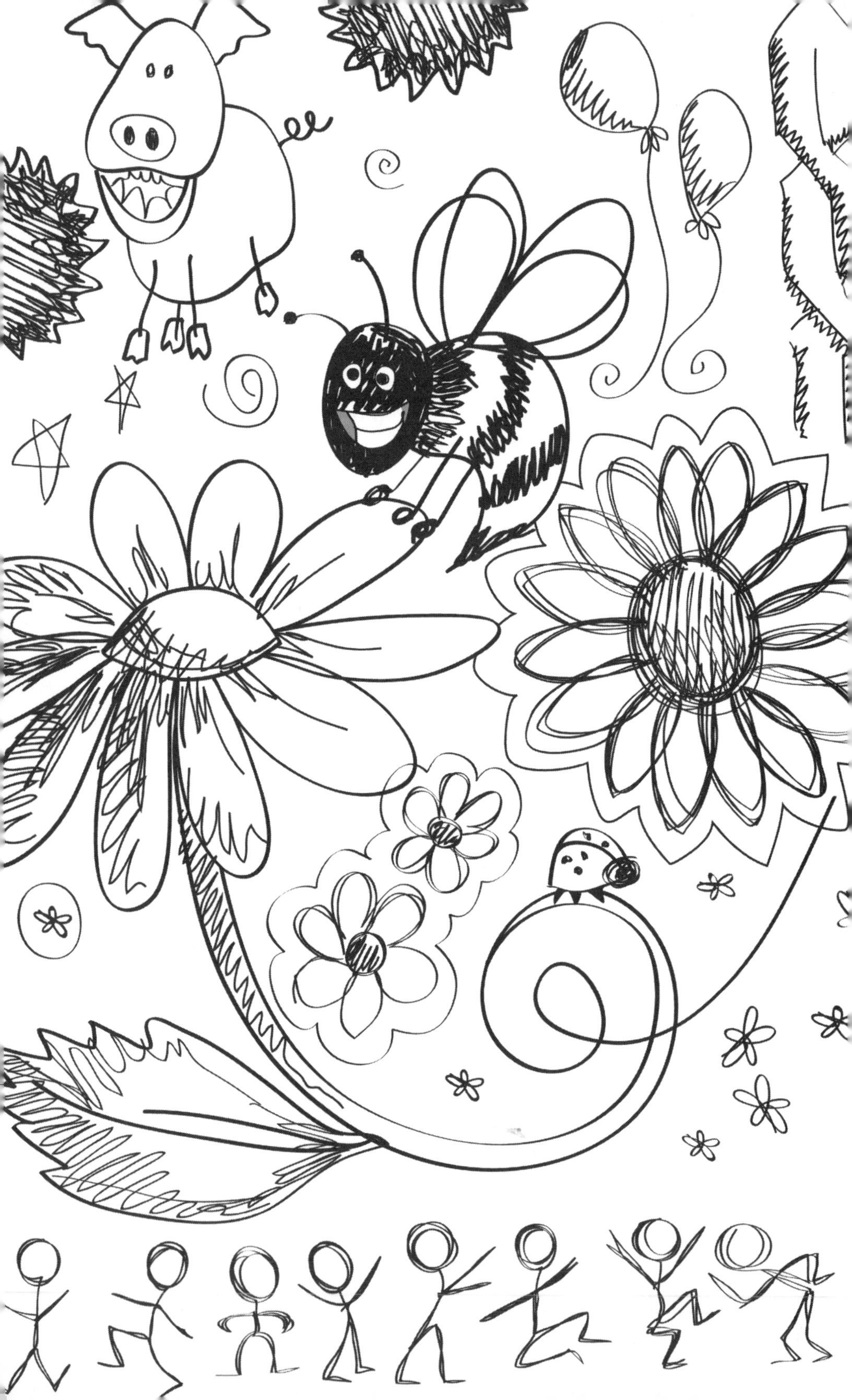

BAD NEWS, THE SEQUEL

OK, so Jack and I came back to the fort for some quality guy time. We were goofing off, sticking ants onto sappy spots on the tree, when we decided to grab the sketchbook down from the branch so we could write some rules for our new fort.

AS YOU CAN PLAINLY SEE, THIS BOOK HAS BEEN TAMPERED WITH!!!

Apparently, some GIRL thinks she can draw in MY sketchbook. Worse yet, she discovered our fort.

Jack was the one who found the new drawings. He opened the sketchbook and said, "What's with you and the flowers? That's dumb."

He held out the page for me to see. I grabbed the sketchbook and plopped onto the cushion, my head spinning and my mouth agape.*

"Those aren't my drawings," I said. "Apparently some girl has broken into our fort. She probably sat her girly self down on this very fort futon and read this book. Then—BLECH!—she drew in it!"

"At least she didn't drink our sodas," said Jack.

Normally I would agree—sodas <u>are</u> ultra-important—but SHE DREW IN MY SKETCHBOOK!

"Who do you think did it?" I asked. "A billion girls live around here... Ew! What if a whole gang of girls was in our fort...combing each other's hair and talking about High School Musical and stuff?"

"No idea who did it. I never pay attention to any of them," said Jack matter-of-factly. And it's true, we don't notice girls much. We're always too busy having our own fun. "Let's just rip that page out," he added.

That had occurred to me too—we could tear out the girly page and be done with it.

But first of all, the page has a couple of MY drawings on the other side—the baseball diamond masterpiece and Show-off Girl.

Second of all, why should I have to rip up my sketchbook just because someone ELSE messed with it?

And third of all, something about the drawings gave me a bubbly, curious feeling...

PLUS... I'D HATE TO WASTE THE PAPER. I MEAN, THE DRAWINGS AREN'T TERRIBLE OR ANYTHING.

"No," I said. "I want to figure out who's to blame, and we might need the drawings as evidence. How are we going to identify her—or them?"

"Let's show it to Sasha," said Jack. "She might know."

Sasha is the girl who lives next door to Jack's Dad-house. She's two grades older. We DO talk to Sasha once in a while, because she's nearby and sometimes gives us popsicles.

Then I realized that showing the girly drawings to Sasha probably meant showing her the whole sketchbook, which made my stomach flip. Then word would surely get back to Tommy Geller, who'd torment me for the rest of my life.

THE MIGHTY GEEK IS AT IT AGAIN! THIS TIME IT'S FLOWERS, BOYS AND GIRLS!

"Ummm...I think I have a better plan," I said. "Let's put the sketchbook back in the tree...and go see Mr. Mot."

THE STAKE-OUT

We stashed the sketchbook back in the crook of the tree and went to talk to Mr. Mot. He can see the pine tree from his front porch.

"Hello, boys," said Mr. Mot. "It's an ambrosial* evening, with the alluring* aroma of apple blossoms in the air—agreed?"

ALLITERATION* ALERT!

"Sure, Mr. Mot," I said. "Whatever you say. Hey, did you see any girls by that tree over there?"

"Now that you mention it, I did see a red-head there earlier today. Why?"

I glanced at Jack. "Umm...we're making a fort, and we think someone messed with our stuff," he said.

"What 'stuff'?" said Mr. Mot. "And why do you assume* it was a girl?" Mr. Mot is old, but he's still sharp.

"We found a barrette," I lied. "...and...a doll...and a shiny pink purse."

OK, maybe I went too far with the pink purse, but I really didn't want to have to explain my latest sketchbook problems. Jack looked at me askance.*

"Is it OK if Jack and I hide behind your bushes and see if anyone goes into our fort?" I asked.

"I suppose there's no harm in that," said Mr. Mot. "I'll go call your parents and let them know you're here." Good old Mr. Mot. Always looking out for our safety.

So Jack and I crouched behind Mr. Mot's shrubs and settled in for a stake-out. We whispered for a while about girls with red hair. Did we know any girls with red hair? We couldn't think of any.

Actually, Jack and I realized we couldn't recall the hair color of <u>any</u> girls (except our moms, and they're not girls—they're <u>relatives</u>).

As it began to get dark, we strained to keep watching the fort across the street, but there was no movement. "Wish we had some snacks," I muttered. "Don't guys on stake-outs usually have snacks? Like doughnuts or something?"

Who ever heard of a stealth operation with no snacks? I need my energy. Sheesh.

THIS WOULD BE ME IF I ATE AS MANY OF MY DAD'S FAMOUS SNICKERDOODLES AS I WANTED.

Jack dug in his pocket and pulled out a fistful of pebbles and two old Tootsie Rolls. "Better than nothin'," he said, and I was thinking the same thing, but then he unwrapped his and fed it to Slate, so I had to give mine to Max.

TOOTSIE ROLL VANILLA FLAVORED

Max curled up next to me, and Slate curled up next to Jack. Pretty soon Slate was asleep, then Max was asleep, and next time I looked, Jack was asleep too. So I woke everyone up and we headed home. On the way, I crawled under the tree and got the sketchbook. I kind of need it with me, you know?

COUCH MONEY

Jack and I are Slushie aficionados.* Almost every day during the summer, we bike to the convenience store down the street for a little frozen refreshment.

Cola

Mango-Passion Fruit

Bubble Gum

Cola

Diet Lemon (Big Mistake)

Exxtreem Blue Razz

Cola

All in all, this Slushie is about a 7.5 out of 10.

My mom and dad give me an allowance on Fridays, and it's enough to buy small Slushies throughout the week—but barely. If I want to get some chips or candy, too, I come up short in just a few days. So I have to augment* my income with couch money.

Couch money is money that falls out of grown-ups' pockets and gets lost in furniture cushions. It's usually coins, but once in a while it's a dollar bill.

To find couch money, you stick your arms deep down into the slots near the arms and backs of chairs and couches, then you pull out whatever you can feel. In my house, lots of times it's trash—candy wrappers, trading card packages, sticky straws. Where does all that stuff come from, anyway?

64 CENTS AND A FOSSILIZED FRENCH FRY! NOT BAD FOR A MORNING'S WORK!

UM, LET ME TAKE A LOOK AT THAT...

Usually I find a coin or two in a chair, and maybe five or six in a couch. When I have enough money for a Slushie, I'm done couch-diving for the day. But the next day, I have to find a new spot to try. Junk drawers are good. The car can be a goldmine. And this week, while Timothy is still gone, the floor in his room has LOTS of potential.

THE AIRPLANE POSTER IS ASKEW.*

This afternoon Jack and I went to buy Slushies, and when we got to the convenience store, some girls were in the Slushie line ahead of us.

WHAT DO YOU KNOW...
NOW THAT I'M PAYING ATTENTION,
THEY <u>DON'T</u> REALLY ALL LOOK THE SAME...
WEIRD.

"Do you know any of those girls?" whispered Jack.

"I've seen the one with blackish hair and a pink stripe before," I whispered back. Guess I didn't speak quietly enough. Pink-stripe girl looked back and gave me the evil eye.

After we got our Slushies, we put them in the water bottle holders on our bikes—boy, those sure come in handy—and rode up and down the streets of our neighborhood. We were looking for girls with red hair. We've never looked for girls before. Sheesh. It was appalling.*

We saw girls playing hopscotch, girls running through sprinklers, girls selling lemonade, even one girl climbing high in a tree—but no girls with red hair.

"Where else can we spy on girls?" I asked Jack.

"When we go swimming, there are always girls at the pool," he said.

"There are?" I said. "OK, let's go swimming."

So that's where we're going next, after we relax in the fort for a few minutes and finish our Slushies. When I go home to put on my swim trunks, I'll stick the sketchbook back under my bed, where it'll be safe.

GIRLS, GIRLS EVERYWHERE

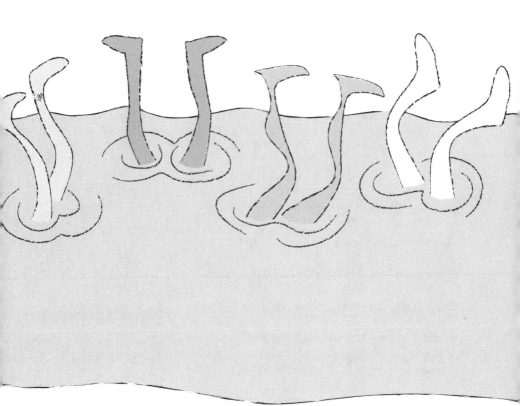

When Jack and I got to the pool, we forgot all about looking for girls and started playing our usual swimming games: who can hold his breath the longest and who can lie on the hot cement the longest.

For breath-holding, sometimes we just stick our heads underwater at the same time and see who pops up first. But usually we combine it with another skill, such as diving-to-the-bottom-of-the-pool-to-grab-the-rock. When the lifeguard's not looking, Jack throws two rocks into the deep end, and on the count of three, we dive in. You have to grab a rock, swim to the surface, AND stay underwater the longest to win. I plug my nose with my fingers when I'm underwater, and it's hard to swim to the bottom that way. So Jack usually wins.

(BUT I'M PRETTY SURE IT'S THE ROCKS IN HIS POCKETS THAT ARE GIVING JACK AN UNFAIR ADVANTAGE.)

Anyway, it doesn't really matter if Jack is a good sinker, because I RULE at the hot cement game. Here's how it goes: Jack and I swim until we're good and wet and Jack's lips are a little purple from the cold, then we lie down—with no towels—on the sunniest patch of cement we can find. It feels good at first, but in about 30 seconds, if it's a really hot day, Jack starts to squirm like a kernel of microwave popcorn.

Today, while we were lying there on the cement, a clump of girls walked in front of us and blocked our sun. That's the only reason we noticed them.

"Hey, those are girls," said Jack.

So I casually stood up, stretched, draped my towel over my shoulders, and ambled* to the water fountain. As I leaned to drink, I turned my head in the direction of the girls. Sure enough, one of them had red hair! Well, kind of red hair...brownish-reddish. Like a Colorado squirrel.

I was just wondering *Now what?* when Tommy Geller strolled by and stepped hard—accidentally on purpose*—on my foot.

OH, WHOOPS. DIDN'T SEE YOU THERE, MG. YOU SHOULD BE MORE CAREFUL WHERE YOU STAND.

"OWWWWW!" I screamed. It REALLY hurt. It hurt so much that I had to sit down to rub my foot, and my eyes started to water, so I had to cover my face with my towel.

IT WAS JUST SO SUNNY, YOU KNOW? SOME SUN, OR SUNSCREEN, OR A BUG GOT IN MY EYE.

When I looked up again, Tommy was standing there with a fake look of concern on his face. "You okay, MG?" he asked.

The girls had come closer to see what was wrong. They were forming a circle around me. Then the one with squirrely-red hair stepped forward and said, "Do you need me to get you a bandaid or ice pack or something? I live right across the street."

MG. HIS NAME IS MG? WHAT DOES THAT STAND FOR?

MIGHTY GEEK. I HEARD IT'S BECAUSE HE COLLECTS STUFFED UNICORNS.

I didn't know what to do or say. I wanted to punch Tommy Geller, and I wanted to ask Squirrel Girl if she messed with my sketchbook, but mostly I wanted to be alone.

So I said nothing. I just stood and marched home. When I left, Jack was diving for rocks. I don't think he even saw what happened.

Next time, this is what I'm gonna do to Tommy Geller:

BOOGER POTION

Today Jack and I forgot about our girl troubles for a while and made a potion. My dad likes to cook, and he let us take a bunch of his ingredients from the kitchen cupboards and refrigerator. We mixed them together in an empty mayonnaise jar.

We started with mustard and cinnamon and green food coloring. We added some Tabasco sauce, baking soda, sugar, and this black stuff called Liquid Smoke that smells like a campfire. We cracked in an egg and threw in a handful of chocolate chips. Then we sprinkled in about twenty more things, filled the rest of the jar up with water, screwed on the lid, and shook it.

EGG YUCK...
I MEAN YOLK.

GUMMY WORM

HEADLESS
GUMMY WORM

COFFEE BEANS,
DECAF ONES

JACK'S ROCK

Our potion was disgusting. It was awesome.
It was disgustingly awesome. It was mostly
brown, but you could see egg yolk and coffee beans
and chocolate chips swirling around inside.

"I dare you to taste it," Jack said.

"I dare both of us to taste it," I said.

We decided that the only fair way
would be for us each to get a spoonful and
put the spoons into each other's mouths at the
exact same millisecond.

On the count of three, we shoved in the
spoons.

Right away Jack made such a bug-eyed,
squinched-up face that I started to snort-laugh.
That made the potion come shooting out my nose,
which was kind of a good thing because I couldn't
taste it as much.

But it was a bad thing, too, because now I
had brown booger-potion dribbled down the front of
my shirt.

"Guhross!" said Jack.

I made a booger-monster face, raised up my arms over my head, formed my hands into claws, and growled at Jack.

THE POTION JAR LID IS AJAR.*

Maybe I could scare Squirrel Girl into telling me the truth if I booger-monstered her! Nah. That's dumb.

LOOSY GOOSY

Goosy rode her bike to our house today and invited me to go for a ride.

"C'mon, Aldo," she said. "I'll race you to the corner."

I was sitting on the porch swing, minding my own business. "Uh........no," I said. Unless you're going to get a Slushie, biking is one of those hot, sweaty activities I was talking about.

Goosy zigzagged around the driveway on her bike while I creaked back and forth on the swing. She's the kind of grandma who never sits still.

Then she stopped and leaned in close. "I'll treat you to Walrus..."

Walrus is my favorite ice cream shop in the entire universe. I planted my feet and stopped swinging so I could consider the offer. "How long will it take to get there?"

"It's not too far," she said.

"How far is not too far?"

"Oh, just up the bike trail a ways, then across into town."

"Will it take more than half an hour?" Half an hour I could handle, I was thinking. Tops.

"Depends how fast you pedal, Aldo."

"OK," I decided. I yelled to Dad where I was going, strapped on my helmet, and climbed onto my bike.

Goosy beat me to the corner, but after that, she rode behind me into town. And it was far... very, ultra, mega, über far.

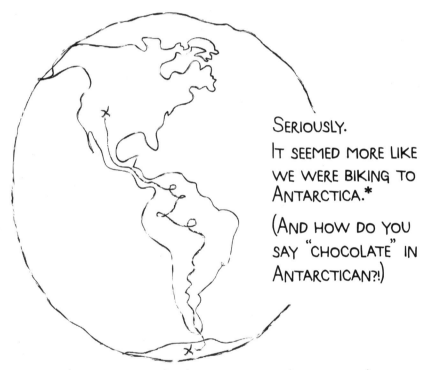

SERIOUSLY.
IT SEEMED MORE LIKE WE WERE BIKING TO ANTARCTICA.*
(AND HOW DO YOU SAY "CHOCOLATE" IN ANTARCTICAN?!)

Three times I had to stop and rest, and once I even had to pretend to tip over next to the path so I could lie down in the grassy shade for a few minutes.

When we FINALLY got to Walrus, Goosy chose a waffle cone with Banana ice cream, and I picked Oreo with Oreos on top. We each got three cherries.

"I'm making a gigantic painting," she said as she licked her cone.

Goosy really is a painter. She has even sold some of her paintings in art galleries.

"It's taller than I am. It's a painting of Horsetooth Rock, but I'm afraid it looks more like an anthill at this point."

Horsetooth Rock is a famous mountain at the edge of our town. People say it looks like a row of horse's teeth, but to me it looks more like giant steps in a Mario game.

JUMPING ON ZE HORSE'S ATEETH! ITSA DISGUSTING!

"So how's your sketchbook coming along?" she asked. One thing about Goosy, even when she's sitting still, her eyes are still dancing.

I shrugged. "It's OK, I guess." *OK except that some girl invaded it.*

"What are you drawing?"

"Comics."

"Audacious!* Are you having fun with it?"

I thought about how my hand feels when I draw—like it knows what it's doing. I also thought about how I feel both good and bad—ambivalent*— about being artsy-fartsy. "Kinda."

"That's what matters, you know."

"Do you have fun when you paint, Goosy?"

"Yes, gobs of fun. I have so much fun that sometimes I paint all day and all night, and I lose track of time. But it can be kind of scary, too, knowing other people are going to look at my paintings."

Hm. I knew exactly what she meant. I don't want to show my sketchbook to lots of people, either. It's kind of private.

IF I WANTED TO BE MADE FUN OF, I WOULD BE DRAWING UNICORNS ON THE SIDEWALK INSTEAD.

(PROUDLY DRAWN BY ALDO ZELNICK)

"If you feel like sharing your drawings with me someday, I'd like to see them," said Goosy, and she winked at me.

But before I could tell her maybe, Goosy was standing up and buckling on her helmet. "Time for me to get back to my anthill!" she sang.

I groaned. "Let's call Dad and see if he'll come pick us up."

"Pish-posh," said Goosy. "Put your mettle to the pedal, boy."

So we biked...all...the....way....home, and somehow I lived to draw about it.

DON'T WORRY! I'M AN ICE-CREAMATARIAN!

SQUIRREL GIRL

Since we know approximately* where Squirrel Girl lives, Jack and I decided to hang out near her house today. Our plan was to walk up and down the sidewalk, pretending to be looking for rocks and stuff, until we saw her.

I was wearing my backpack, and the sketchbook was inside it.

YUP. JUST TAKING ADVANTAGE OF THIS BEAUTIFUL DAY TO GET SOME FRESH AIR AND SAY HELLO TO MY NEIGHBORS!

Hard to believe, but our plan actually worked! I was just starting to feel ridiculous when Squirrel Girl came shuffling out of one of the houses dressed in a swimsuit and flip-flops. She had a towel wrapped around her neck.

She even recognized me. "Hey, you're the kid who got hurt at the pool the other day."

"Uh, yeah." That's when I realized I hadn't planned what to say to her about the sketchbook.

Just then Jack spoke up. "So, your hair is kinda red," he said. "Do you like to draw?"

AWKWARD!*

"Uh...a little, I guess," she said. She was definitely looking askance at us now. "Why?"

"Because someone drew in my...notebook," I said. Calling it a notebook suddenly seemed a tiny bit less geeky. "And we're trying to figure out who."

"Let me see it," she said. I appreciated her directness. She seemed nice, and honest.

So I got my sketchbook out of my backback and opened it to the flower drawings. She gave the girly page a quick glance and said, "Oh yeah, that's really good. I can't draw like that. Gotta go!" And she flip-flopped off in the direction of the swimming pool.

Jack and I sat down on the curb. "She's not our girl," Jack said.

"Nope." I felt kind of let down. I thought for sure it was her.

DON'T SAY 'OUR GIRL.' THAT'S SUPER-DUMB.

"Oh well. Let's play Monopoly," said Jack.

That's not as arbitrary* as it sounds. Jack and I have been on a Monopoly kick lately.

"OK, but I get to be Obi-Wan," I said. Jack's mom got him a Star Wars Monopoly set on eBay last week.

As Jack and I walked to his Mom-house, I made a mental note to show Goosy my sketchbook. Maybe she'll help us figure out how to find artsy girl.

GOODIES FOR GRANDMA

I helped my dad make snickerdoodles this morning. They're these really buttery, cinnamony cookies. You roll the dough into little balls then put them on baking sheets. In the oven, the balls flatten into delicious circles.

Dad likes to cook all kinds of things, but he especially likes to bake. He bakes cakes and pies and cinnamon rolls. He always makes the birthday cakes in my family. And once in a while he even bakes fancy wedding cakes for friends when they get married.

(BAKING ISN'T DAD'S JOB...IT'S JUST SOMETHING HE DOES FOR FUN.)

While we were mixing the dough, Dad talked to me about baseball.

"Are you having fun playing?"

"Not really," I said.

"Hm. I wonder why not?"

"Cause I ~~stink~~ am abysmal* at sports."

Dad got this sad look on his face then, which made me feel kinda sad.

"I can't help it I'm not athletic," I said. "I was born like this!"

GOO GOO GAMECUBE!

"I was never athletic either, Aldo," Dad admitted. "But your mom and I want you to try some different things until you find a sport you do like. It's more about attitude* than aptitude,*" he added. "If you believe you're going to have fun playing baseball, then you will."

Attitude, schmattitude, I thought.

"Here, take these to Goosy," he said, handing me a basket of still-warm cookies. "They're her favorite."

So I called Jack and we walked to Goosy's house. She paints in a huge, sunny, windowy room in the back, and that's where we found her.

Wow. She wasn't kidding when she said her new painting was gigantic.

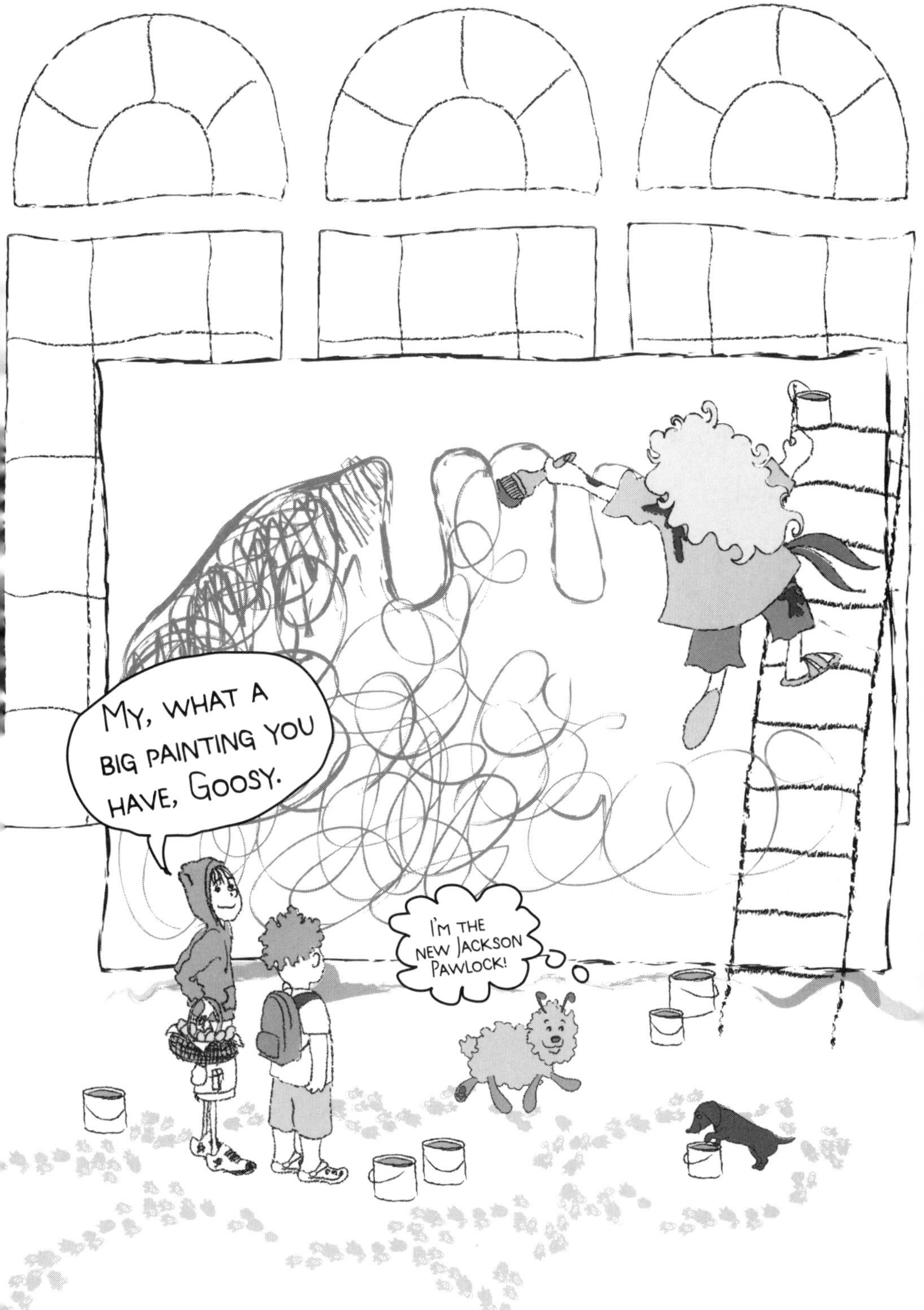
MY, WHAT A BIG PAINTING YOU HAVE, GOOSY.
I'M THE NEW JACKSON PAWLOCK!

"Dad and I made you some cookies!" I yelled up to her.

"Oh goody!" she said, and she came down from her ladder.

We sat at a little table in her studio and ate the cookies. "Mmmmmm," Goosy said. She had snickerdoodle crumbs on her face. "So, what do you think of my painting?"

"It's colorful," said Jack, leaning back in his chair to get a better look. "But pegmatite isn't really purple."

"It's big," I said.

"The better to make you feel small," she said, waggling her eyebrows at us. "I'm trying to capture what it's like when I hike up to Horsetooth Rock. I feel like I don't matter so much, but the mountain does."

("Are Goosy's eyes always this big?" Jack whispered to me. "And her teeth, too?")

I ignored Jack. "I brought my sketchbook to show you," I told Goosy.

She jumped to her feet and clapped her hands. "Wonderful!" she cried.

This startled Jack. His chair tipped backwards with him in it.

Goosy hoisted up Jack by his red hoodie, then dipped a fat brush into the paint and handed it to me.

"Go paint some of my rock while I enjoy your sketchbook," she said.

So I climbed the ladder and tried to imitate Goosy's brushstrokes. Normally I'm a little acrophobic*, but it was fun being up there, wildly dabbing purple on such a huge canvas. While I painted, Jack crouched beneath the ladder. I don't know why he was acting so weird.

"Why Aldo!" Goosy was exclaiming from below. "Your drawings are marvelous! The comics are not only apt*, they're funny! I look just like me!"

"They're not that good," I called down. "They're OK." But inside I was happy. Turns out it feels good to have someone admire your artsy-fartsyness.

My brush was running out of paint. "Did you notice the stupid flowers?" I asked Goosy as I climbed down.

I explained to her how I had left the sketchbook in my fort overnight and found the girly drawings the next day. I also told her about our search for the redhead.

"My," she said. "This is indeed a mystery. I can tell you that every artist has a style. If you could somehow see samples of their work, you could probably identify her."

Jack and I got ready to go. Goosy smiled her toothy smile and wrapped both me and Jack into one big hug. "Toodle-oo!" she said. "Thanks for the cookies! Come back and paint with me sometime soon!"

"Man," said Jack as we hurried home. (For some reason he wanted to get away quickly.) "She's not your ordinary grandmother."

"Nope," I said. "She's Goosy."

AMERICA'S PASTIME*

It's tomorrow. I'm in the fort, recovering from my team's first baseball game.

Have you ever noticed that baseball has absurdly complicated rules? I mean, in soccer, you try to kick the ball into the other team's net. Simple as pie. ⟶ Basketball's the same, except you throw the ball instead of kicking it. (Not that I'd want to play either of those sports, because you're running full-speed the whole time, but still.)

With baseball, all nine players take the field and stand in random spots and do random things, depending on where the ball is hit and how many outs there are. Who can keep track of what's going on?

OH GEEZ.
Now I'M DRAWING FLOWERS.

But the biggest problem is that in my league, anyway, the ball almost never gets hit.

The pitcher pitches the ball to the catcher, and the catcher throws it back to the pitcher, and this happens ad nauseum*, until us fielders get so bored we forget we're playing baseball and start picking dandelions instead.

Which is what I was doing in right field tonight when some bruiser of a kid on the other team hit a fly ball.

I had just picked a dandelion and was playing that game where you flick the dandelion flower off its stem as you chant, "Mama had a baby and its HEAD popped off."

You're supposed to flick the flower right
when you say the word *head*. It's tricky to get
the flicking and the timing just right, though, so
I was concentrating pretty hard when, out of the
corner of my ear, I heard people yelling, "Aldo! Aldo!
Aldooooooo!"

I looked up just in time to notice that my
teammates, my coach, and my family were all
staring at me, and some of them were pointing up
in the air.

So I looked up, raised my glove to the sky, and tried desperately to find the ball. (Where is it, where is it, where is it?) Oh! I saw it! By some miracle, I saw the round white ball with red laces spinning straight down to my glove! (YESSSS! I RULE at baseball!) Oh, wait.

I STARTED WONDERING:

WHY DID IT SEEM LIKE THE BALL JUST KEPT GETTING BIGGER AND BIGGER?

AND THEN IT HIT ME.

That's right. I must have misjudged it by a smidge.

The ball whizzed past my glove and hit me smack on the right eye. Next thing you know, I was sitting with my parents in the stands, holding an ice pack to my face.

Now my eye is puffy and sore and starting to turn purple.

Did I mention I HATE baseball and I'm never playing it again?

I'm leaving the sketchbook here in the fort again for the night. I brought a lunchbox to put it in so it won't get wrecked if it rains.

NOTE TO GIRL:

If you're reading this, it means you broke into our fort again. Stop drawing in my sketchbook.

But if you do, tell us who you are.

Drumroll,
please...

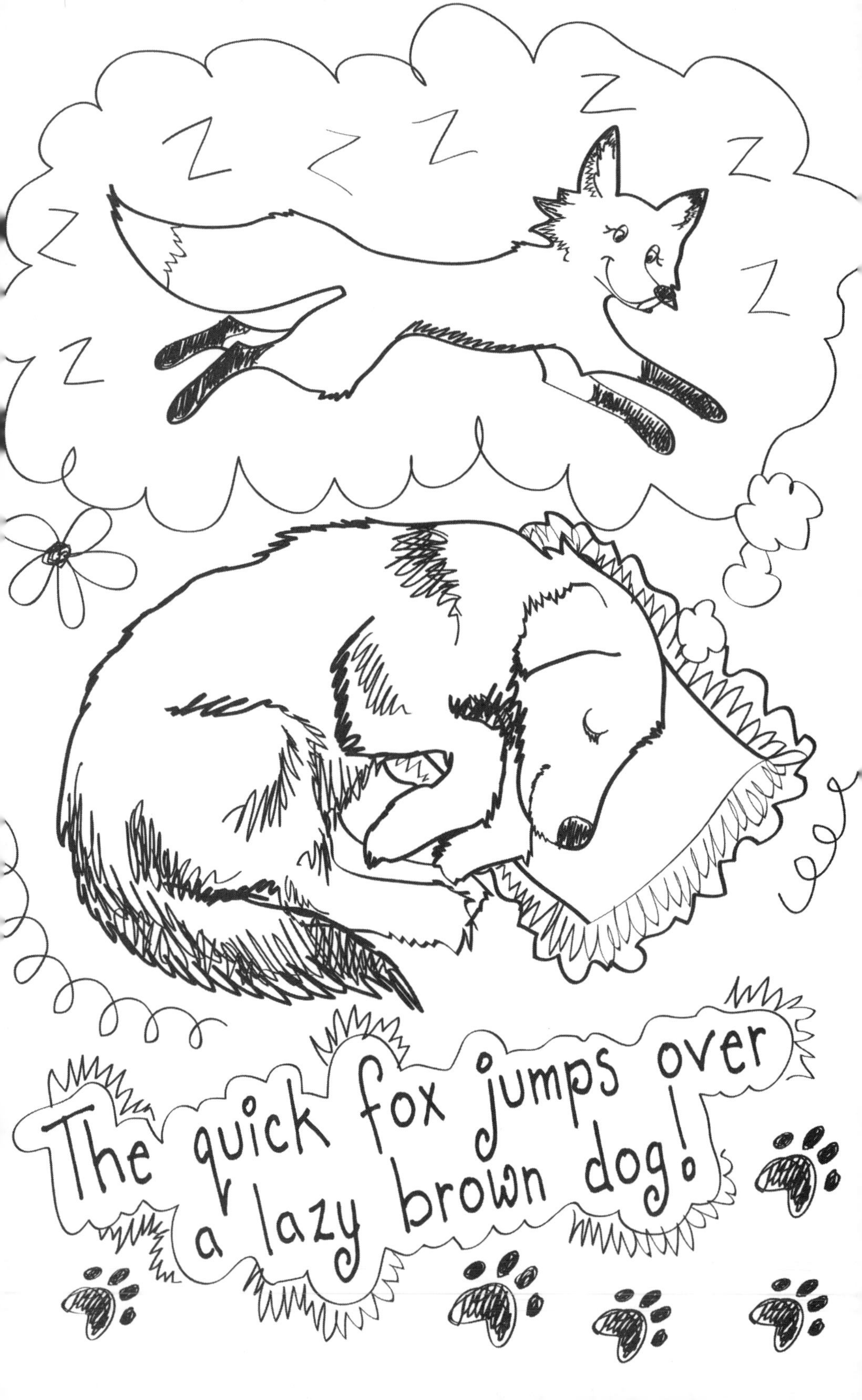
The quick fox jumps over
a lazy brown dog!

Asparagus*
Broccoli
Citrus
Dragonfly
Elephant
Foothills
Garden
Horsetooth!

A

pretty pictures by "Anonymous*"

ALIEN* INVADER!

Oho! Now this is really taking things a bit too far.

Jack and I returned to the fort to check the sketchbook for new clues and found not one but <u>two</u> pages chock-full of girl doodles.

What the heck?

I asked her to reveal her identity, but no... she just ran amuck* with cutesy animals and weird vegetables in my sketchbook. Jack says she must be a vegetarian, but that's dumb. No kid actually <u>likes</u> vegetables. So what's up with the giant asparagus?

And the handwriting...Jack pointed out how it curls and swoops. Now we know that the mystery artist <u>has to be</u> a girl.

We're going to go ask Mr. Mot if he got a better look at her this time.

MR. MOT
TO THE RESCUE

Jack and I had just crawled out from under the tree and were crossing to Mr. Mot's house when guess who came around the corner towards us?

Yup, my archenemy,* Tommy Geller. And he wasn't alone. His gang of bullies was at his side.

And there I was, carrying this sketchbook.

Yes, the sketchbook that actually says "Red Letter Sketchbook" on the cover—just so there's no confusion that it can only be for DRAWING PICTURES!

"Hey, MG and MG's scrawny friend!" he said, sounding happy to see us. He glanced at his buddies with a look that meant *Here's somethin' to do, fellas.*

Jack and I kept walking, and I tried to hide the sketchbook behind my back, but Tommy stepped in front of me. "Whatcha got there, MG?"

I turned to Jack. Jack is usually an amiable* guy, but I was hoping he would come up with something tough to say. Jack looked Tommy Geller straight in the eye and said, "I'm sorry you feel the need to be such a bully."

Once again, <u>AWKWARD!</u>

Tommy's eyebrows crunched together and his face began turning watermelon-Slushie red. "Lemme see that book," he said.

What could I do? I couldn't outrun them.
And Tommy could easily grab the sketchbook away
from me.

So I did the only sensible thing I could do. I
stuffed it down the back of my pants and yelled at
the top of my lungs.

HELPHELPHELPHELPHELPHELP

YUCK. NOT WORTH IT.

GOOD ONE, ALDO!

My yelling brought Mr. Mot out into the street. "Is there a problem, gentlemen?" he asked.

Tommy and his friends backed away. After all, Mr. Mot had been a teacher. Kids still respond to his teacherish authority.*

SMARTER THAN A LIBRARIAN, MORE AUTHORITATIVE THAN A GRAMMARIAN. ABLE TO STRING GOBS OF COMPLICATED WORDS TOGETHER IN A SINGLE SENTENCE... IT'S A PROFESSOR! IT'S A PRINCIPAL! No, IT'S MR. MOT!

"Whoa, thanks, Mr. Mot," I said. "That was close." My heart was still pounding a little. "We were just coming to see you. We wondered if you saw a girl near our fort again."

I pulled the sketchbook out of my pants and wiped it on my shirt.

("What, did you fart on it?" whispered Jack.)

"Oh, you've been keeping up with your writing!" said Mr. Mot, who either hadn't heard Jack or was pretending he hadn't. "Well done."

"Yeah, well, someone else has been writing in it too," I said. "Look." And I showed Mr. Mot the latest girlyness.

"Yes, I would say that is indeed the handiwork of a young female," said Mr. Mot.

"You told us you saw a redhead in our fort," I said, "but the only redheaded girl we can find in our neighborhood isn't the one."

"Ahhhh," said Mr. Mot. "You assumed I meant red hair. I did indeed spy a redhead under your tree, but of a different sort. The girl I saw had a red head because she was wearing a red hat."

I CAN'T HELP HOW MY BODY RESPONDS TO FEAR! SHEESH!

"Ohhhhhhhhhh," Jack and I said together. A red hat. Finally a new break in the case.

THE RETURN OF SUPER-JOCK (A.K.A.* TIMOTHY)

Dad and I are going to Denver today to pick up Timothy from baseball camp. The drive takes an hour, which is boring, but we're stopping for lunch. Catch ya later!

OK, I'm back. On the way to Denver, Dad and I went to the best restaurant <u>ever</u>. We had cheeseburgers, onion rings, and malts, which came in giant metal cups.

Then we picked up Timothy, who looked really happy to see me. He gave me a hug and lifted me off the ground. He didn't even call me "chub" like he sometimes does.

On the way home, Timothy told us all about baseball camp, and I told him all about my baseball team.

I brought the sketchbook in the car to show to Timothy. He liked the Super-Jock bit, although he strongly disagrees that if you chase a ball around you're a nitwit. And he wanted to know how much money I found on the floor of his room. (Dang. I forgot I had put that part in here.)

"Just a few quarters," I said, which was a little white underestimate. It was more like three bucks.

"You owe me a dollar," he said. "What's up with the asparagus?"

So I filled him in on the hunt for the mystery girl.

"Now Jack and I are kind of stuck," I said. "We know that she probably doesn't have red hair...just a red hat. But pretty much everyone in the universe has a red hat."

"True," said Timothy, who was wearing a red hat.

"Goosy says that every artist has a certain style, so we just have to check out the artwork of all the girls in the neighborhood. But how are we supposed to do that?"

"You could have an art contest," shrugged Timothy. "Invite all the kids in the neighborhood to submit a drawing, and you and Jack can be the judges."

"Hey, that's a good idea," I said. "But it sounds like a lot of work."

"OK, here's a simpler idea. Did you notice that your girl left you great samples of her handwriting?"

"Don't say 'your girl,'" I said. "That's asinine.*"

"That sentence she wrote...the quick fox jumps over a lazy brown dog....that's called a pangram. It contains all 26 letters of the alphabet. I know because we had to type pangrams in my keyboarding class last year for practice."

"Cool," I said. I flipped to the asparagus page and sure enough, there are all the letters of the alphabet, right there.

"So all we have to do is get a handwriting sample from all the girls in the neighborhood," he said.

"Oh, is that all," I said. I was thinking that baseball camp had addled* Timothy's brain.

"It'll be easy," he said. "You'll see. I have a plan."

Pangrams for Typing Practice

A quart jar of oil mixed with zinc oxide makes a very bright paint.

Heavy boxes perform quick waltzes and jigs.

Six big juicy steaks sizzled in the pan as five workmen left the quarry.

Jaded zombies acted quaintly but kept driving their oxen forward.

Ebenezer unexpectedly bagged two tranquil aardvarks* with his jiffy vacuum cleaner.

Whenever the black fox jumped, the squirrel gazed suspiciously.

The July sun caused a fragment of black pine wax to ooze on the velvet quilt.

Sixty zippers were quickly picked from the woven jute bag.

The five boxing wizards jump quickly.

TIMOTHY ASSISTS

Today we put Timothy's plan into action.

First we went down to the swimming pool, and Timothy talked to the lifeguard. He told her we wanted to set up a table where kids could sign a petition to have a waterslide added to the pool.

She laughed. "Yes, you can do a petition if you want. But you already know that every kid's going to sign it!"

"That's the idea," said Timothy.

So while Timothy made a sign to hang on the front of the table, Jack and I dragged a folding table down from my house and set up three chairs behind it. We also borrowed clipboards, paper, and pens from my mom.

Timothy is a genius! We got 53 signatures in just a few hours. At least half were girls.

OUR POOL NEEDS A WATERSLIDE.

WATERSLIDE WANTERS UNITE!

Sign here if you think a waterslide should be added to our neighborhood swimming pool.

Your full name	Your address	Your e-mail
Sigrid Waller	550 Red Wing Dr.	sigridcity@yahoo.com
Miles Lira	223 Linden St.	i'm only 4!
L. Engeldinger	976 Conklin Ave.	engeldingry@q.net
DOM TRANCHITELLA	343 YORK WAY	COMICDOM@GMAIL.COM
Dana Nichols	44 Spring Court	littlesis@frii.com
Trey Avuncular	422 Gillette Junction	airforce@comcast.net
Calvin Bennett	577 Rock Springs Dr.	roughrider5@hotmail.com
T. Humphries	33 Summit Street	tomhumphriesguayahoo.com

So we closed shop and took home the petition, thinking for sure we must have caught artist girl, but when we compared all the petition signatures to the handwriting in the sketchbook, nothing matched! We even used Jack's magnifying glass to be sure, but none of the handwriting even came close to the loopy Ys and Gs and the circle-dot Is and Js.

Dag nab it! Now what?

To make matters worse, our phone rang off the hook for the rest of the day—and Mom was none too happy about it.

THIS IS THE PRESIDENT OF THE NEIGHBORHOOD ASSOCIATION. WE DID NOT AUTHORIZE* A PETITION.

IF THIS RAISES OUR HOMEOWNERS' FEES, I'M GOING TO T.P. YOUR HOUSE.

MRS. ZELNICK, ARE YOU REALLY TRYING TO GET A WATERSLIDE FOR THE POOL? BECAUSE I DON'T THINK THAT'S SAFE FOR MY TOMMY.

CAN I TALK TO TIMOTHY OR ALDO? THEY'RE MY HEROES.

BIRD BY BIRD

Today my mom tricked me and Jack into hiking to Horsetooth Rock! I am <u>so</u> not even kidding. She said she was going birding at a place with lots of rocks, and Jack and I should go with her. (Was this punishment for the waterslide incident?)

"Come get some fresh air," Mom said.

I should have known better. "Fresh air" means the same thing as EXERCISE. It's just worded a little more sneakily.

Birding is spotting different kinds of birds. My mom loves it. She takes pictures of them too. I go with her once in a while. It's like being on a stakeout for birds. You have to quietly sneak and crouch while you keep your eyes peeled.

Fortunately, there's usually lots of sitting still, too, as you listen for birdcalls and stare into the tree branches. But not today...

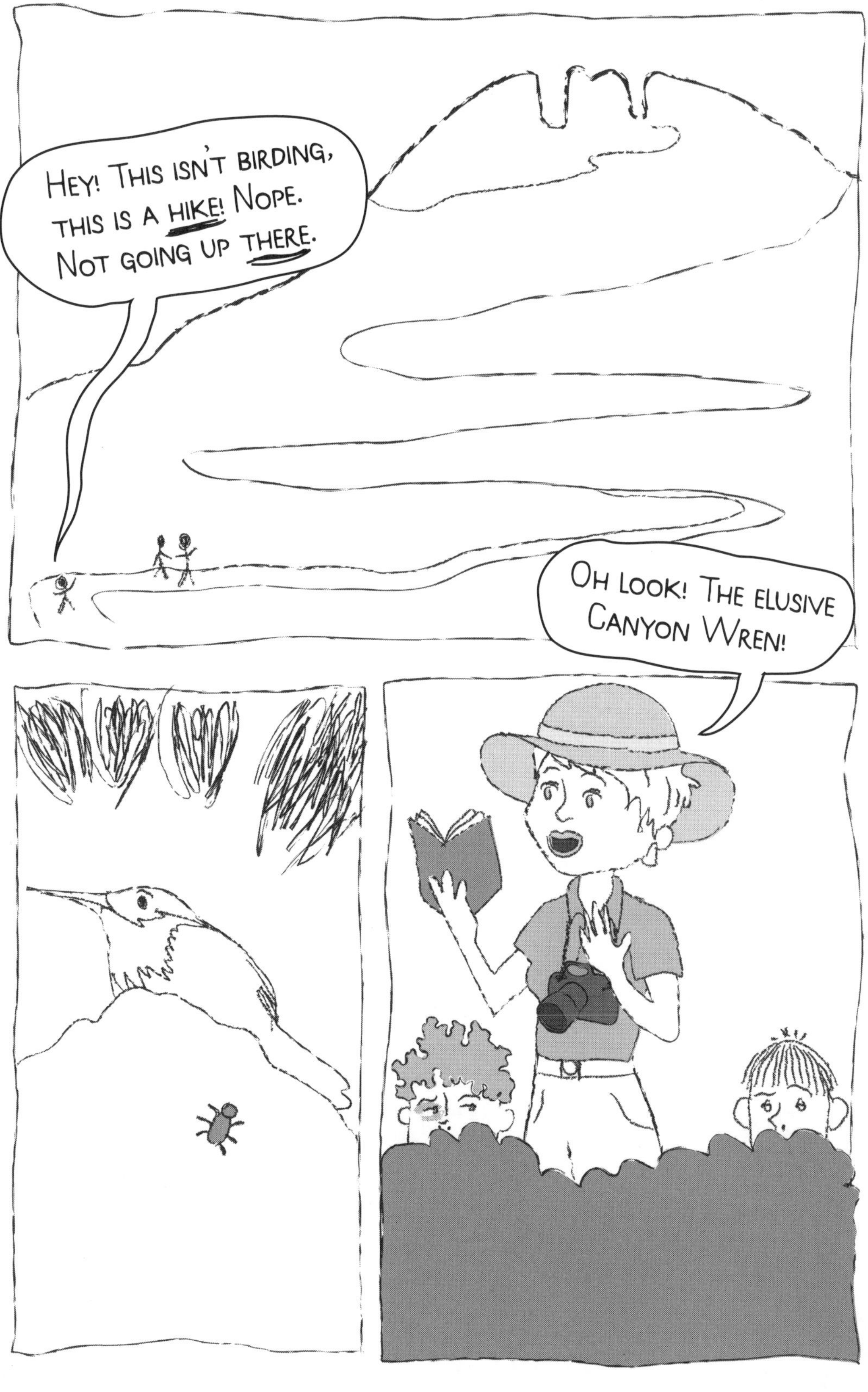
HEY! THIS ISN'T BIRDING, THIS IS A HIKE! NOPE. NOT GOING UP THERE.
OH LOOK! THE ELUSIVE CANYON WREN!

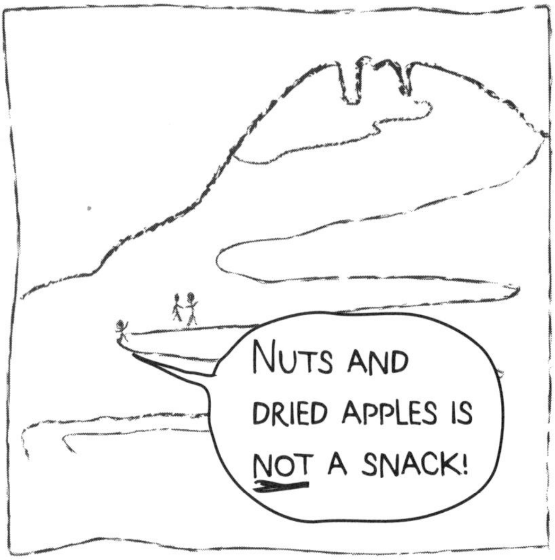
NUTS AND DRIED APPLES IS NOT A SNACK!

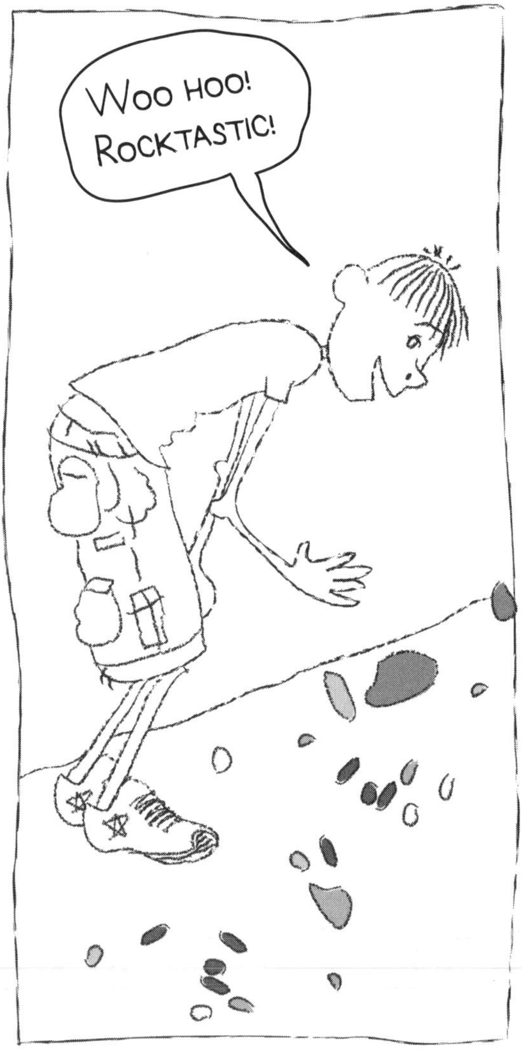
WOO HOO! ROCKTASTIC!

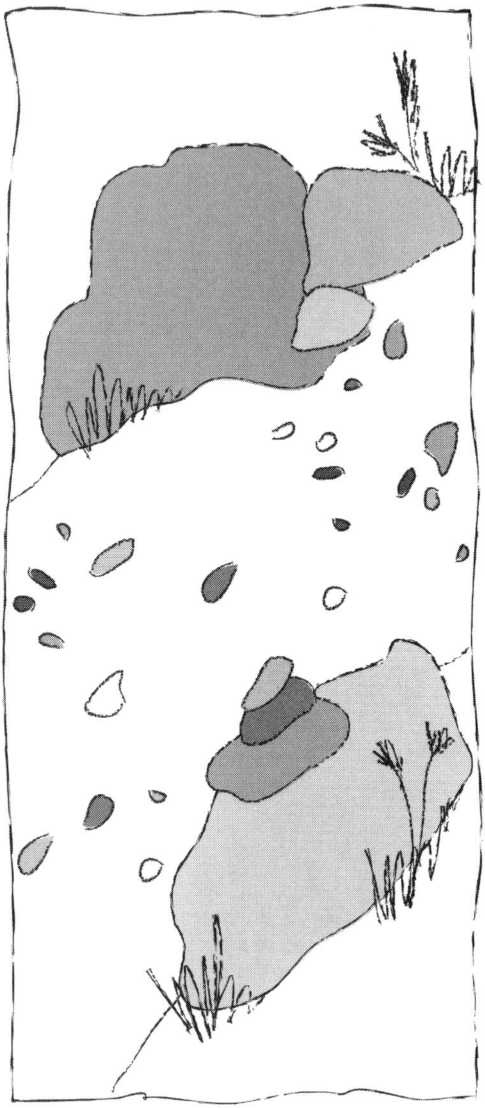

AT LEAST SOME PEOPLE ARE HAVING FUN.

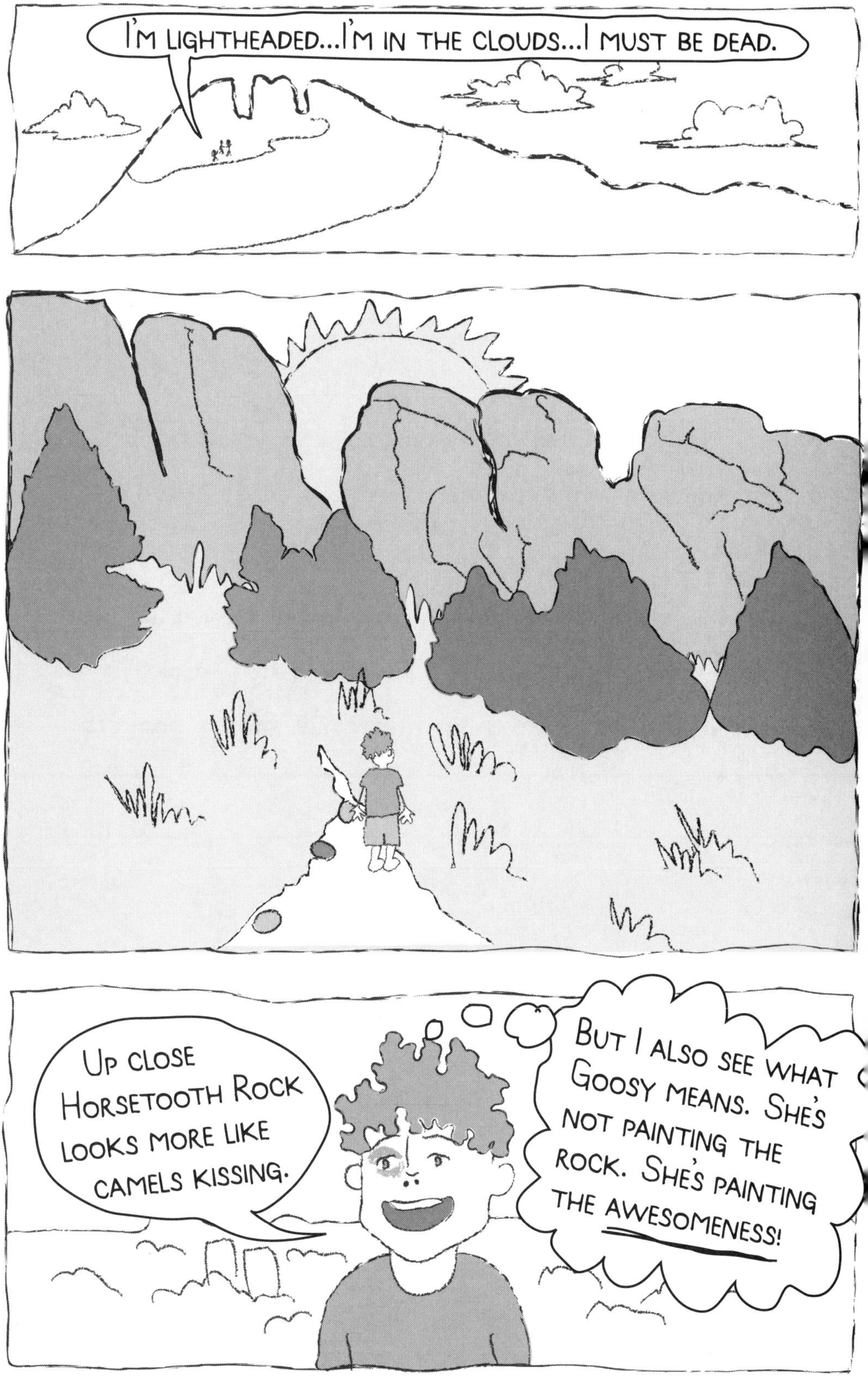
I'M LIGHTHEADED...I'M IN THE CLOUDS...I MUST BE DEAD.
UP CLOSE HORSETOOTH ROCK LOOKS MORE LIKE CAMELS KISSING.
BUT I ALSO SEE WHAT GOOSY MEANS. SHE'S NOT PAINTING THE ROCK. SHE'S PAINTING THE AWESOMENESS!

In the car on the way home from Horsetooth, I thought about the girl who invaded my sketchbook. Does she like to draw in the same way that Jack likes rocks and my mom likes birds? Does it make her feel good, sort of humming with aliveness?

"When we get home, do you want to bike around and look for girls with red hats?" I asked Jack.

"Sure," he said, but I could tell he wasn't really paying attention. He had his new rocks in his lap and was putting them into his shorts pockets by type.

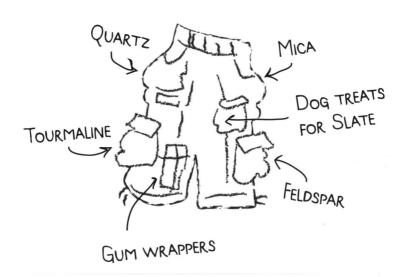

QUARTZ

MICA

DOG TREATS FOR SLATE

TOURMALINE

FELDSPAR

GUM WRAPPERS

"Hey Mom!" I said, realizing that the <u>perfect</u> Slushie opportunity was presenting itself. "We just did a super-hard hike... How about stopping for Slushies?"

My mom looked at me in the rearview mirror and raised one eyebrow, then she smiled. "OK, Aldo, let's stop for Slushies. My treat."

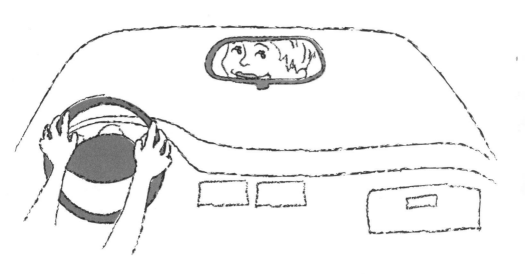

"I'll take two taquitos, too," I said triumphantly.

"Don't push your luck, Zelnick," she said.

OK, OK.

ROCK SHOW

The big rock show was in town today. Once a year, all the professional rock collectors in the area get together and put their best rocks on display. Some of the rocks are just for looking, and some are for sale.

Jack has been looking forward to it for months, and he invited me to go with him.

I've never seen so many special rocks in one place. It was like being in a treasure cave full of sparkling gems, shiny minerals, and just plain cool rocks. Jack was in rock-hound heaven.

SOMEBODY PINCH ME!

Jack's mom, Mrs. Lopez, brought us to the rock show. She and I were walking with Jack from table to table, admiring the rocks as enthusiastically as we could, when who should we bump into but Tommy Geller.

Only this wasn't the tough Tommy Geller from our neighborhood. This was rock-hound Tommy Geller! I could hardly believe my eyes.

I had him right where I wanted him. "Tommy Salami..." I said, cool as a cucumber. "So...you're a rock hound. Who'd have thought? I guess maybe we both have hobbies we'd rather keep quiet about for now, huh?"

Tommy got cherry-Slushie red and nodded. I thought about stomping on his foot, but I opted to take the high road instead. Acting quickly, I borrowed Mrs. Lopez's phone, held it up to Tommy, and took his picture.

"See ya later, Tommynator," I said. "Watch for updates on Facebook."

Before we left, Mrs. Lopez treated us to rock candy on a stick. I chose sour apple flavor, and Jack chose plain. "Plain rock," he said. "Doesn't get any better than this."

"Nope," I had to agree. "It doesn't get any better than this."

SWITCH HITTER

I have some <u>more</u> astonishing,* major-league news, but before I can tell it, I have to explain how it happened.

It all started with batting practice. This afternoon Timothy and I went to the park so I could practice hitting before the big game. (I've gotta admit...Timothy has been suspiciously nice to me since he got home from baseball camp. He either missed me or he broke something of mine, I'm not sure which.)

We took a whole bucket of baseballs and the new red bat Mom let me pick out. The way I figure it, if your mom's forcing you to do an activity you don't really want to do, you should at least get some cool stuff out of it.

I'm not a good hitter, but Timothy was convinced that a little extra batting practice was all I needed. So he pitched me ball after ball after ball, and I swung and missed, swung and missed, swung and missed. Ad nauseum.

"Oh c'mon, Aldo! You ought to be able to hit the cover off the ball," complained Timothy. "Babe Ruth, Kirby Puckett, Tony Gwynn...lots of great hitters were built like you."

Built like you. Remember how I said "fresh air" really means EXERCISE? Well, "built like you" really means CHUBBY.

"Just because you're a Super-Jock doesn't mean I am!" I yelled. "I quit." And I flung my shiny new bat at him.

EVEN AS I'M ATHLETICALLY AVOIDING THE BAT, I'M COMING UP WITH BRILLIANT IDEAS.

"Hey, I know!" he said as he ducked. "You're trying to bat left-handed."

"That's because I AM left-handed, duh!" I was starting to get a little apoplectic.

"Maybe you can bat right-handed! There was a kid at baseball camp who was left-handed, but he batted right-handed!"

"No."

"Try it."

"No!"

"Just once."

"Buy me a Slushie?"

"If you pick up poop." Today was Timothy's day to clean up dog poop in our backyard.

"Deal."

So I switched my hands around on the bat—it felt pretty weird at first—and stood with my left shoulder toward Timothy instead of my right.

Timothy pitched, and I hit the ball...just a little dribbler, but still. I hit it!

He pitched again, and I hit it again.

"You're ambidextrous,* dude!" Timothy said.

I hit a bunch more, then we celebrated with 40-ounce Slushies.

So later on, when my parents brought me to my game, I was actually looking forward to it. Coach put me in right field as usual, but when my team had our ups and it was my turn to bat, I stood confidently, right-handedly, in the batter's box.

The pitcher pitched, and it was just like in the movies, where the ball travels in slow-motion and the batter swings in slow-motion and you just know he's gonna hit the ball out of the park.

Which I didn't. Hit it out of the park, I mean. But I did hit it. The ball rolled between the shortstop's legs, and the left fielder picked it up and threw it over the first base kid's head. It was a triple! I even batted in a run. Abby, the girl on my team, slid into home and scored.

The crowd went wild. Coach high-fived me. Mom, Dad, and Timothy were jumping up and down and cheering. Goosy was doing something that looked a lot like the chicken dance. And Mr. Mot was holding up a sign.

And we haven't even gotten to the astonishing news yet.

That happened after the game, when one of the moms handed me a baseball to sign. You know how kids sometimes sign a baseball to give to their coach as a thank-you present? It was one of those deals.

So I'm signing away, and guess what I see on the baseball? It's a drawing of a little bee with Abby's name written below it. And both the bee and the curly Y look awfully familiar...

Suddenly everything clicked. Red cap, just like the one I was wearing. Bee, short for Abby, just like the bee in the first drawing she made in the sketchbook. I knew her all the time, I just didn't know it!

I had no clue what to do next. I felt kind of mad and kind of shy and a teensy bit glad, all mixed together. Abby walked by me as she was leaving, and I frowned at her and said, "Good slide. But asparagus is uncool."

In my moment of agitation,* that's all I could come up with.

ROCKY MOUNTAIN HIGH

Once or twice every summer, my parents get this crazy idea that we should sleep outdoors—on the cold, rocky ground—and eat food we roast on sticks.

They call it camping.

Dad makes homemade granola bars, Mom packs her birding stuff, Timothy transforms into Super-Camper, and we drive up to the mountains, strap on our backpacks, and hike into the wilderness. Yay.

The hike to Horsetooth Rock was easy compared to this. On the way up, I stepped in a mud-puddle that was 99 percent mud and 1 percent puddle. I sank to my knees, and Dad pulled me out just in time.

Then I <u>thought</u> I caught a glimpse of a bear hiding behind some trees. So I blew my emergency camping whistle, which scared away the rare bird my mom was trying to take a picture of. (Luckily, the bear turned out to be a boulder SHAPED like a bear.)

At least we have a nice, big tent where I can make a tent futon out of all our sleeping bags and read and draw comics while we're here.

Mom said only I would be silly enough to be inside when I'm outside, and she dragged me out of the tent and made me hike around the lake with her and Timothy.

Then Timothy and I had a rock-skipping contest. Guess who won.

Tonight we built a campfire. We had hot dogs for dinner and s'mores for dessert.

Dad told a scary story about a snake in the woods, and Mom sang campfire songs she learned when she was a Girl Scout. Then we all crawled into the tent and got nice and cozy.

HOW AM I SUPPOSED TO GET STARTED DREAMING ABOUT CHEERING CROWDS IF YOU DON'T TURN OFF THAT LIGHT?

I'm using a flashlight to finish this, but Timothy's telling me I have to turn it off. So, good night.

It's morning. Mom's annoyed with me because I could <u>swear</u> I heard a bear in the middle of the night. I heard a growling noise coming from the other side of the tent, and it wasn't Max, because he was inside my sleeping bag with me.

So I blew my emergency whistle again.

Mom sat up and pointed her flashlight at me.

"What's the matter, Aldo!" she whispered, sounding all panicky. "What happened?"

"There's a bear right outside our tent!"

"A bear?"

"Just listen!"

We were both quiet for a second, and there it was again.... "Snrgrr...snrgrrr..."

"See!" I whispered.

"Aldo! That's just your father. Go back to sleep!"

Which I did. But Mom said she couldn't fall asleep again, so she's all tired and grumpy today.

Then when I went outside this morning to look for cool rocks for Jack, I got bitten by about a billion mosquitoes. So now I'm back on my tent futon, enjoying the great outdoors from behind the insect screen.

We're going back to civilization this afternoon...back to my girl troubles. What should I do about Abby?

TO BEE OR NOT TO BEE

I marched over to Bee's house this morning.
I know where she lives because I remember seeing
her climb the tree in her front yard.

I had my sketchbook, and I was ready to be
mad at her. So maybe she can draw. Does that
mean it's OK for her to trespass on my territory?

When I got there, she was in the darned
tree again.

"You drew in my sketchbook," I said. I crossed my arms across my chest and scowled at her.

"I know!" she said. "It was so much fun! It was like a game."

"Hmph. But it's MY sketchbook." I wagged the sketchbook at her. One of Vivi's bubbles landed on it and popped.

"I know it's yours. You're a good artist, Aldo."

Well what was I supposed to say to that? I uncrossed my arms. "Do you like to draw?" I asked. "I mean, is it fun for you?"

"Yes, gobs of fun," she said, and she grinned. "But I have gobs of fun doing lots of things."

"Why aren't you hanging out with other girls?" I asked, realizing she didn't seem to be part of a girl-clump, like most of the others I'd been watching.

"I don't know. I guess I'm not as clumpy as most girls," she said, and she flipped down from the tree then stood on her head.

I sat down a safe distance away from Vivi. Little kids make me nervous. "I tell you what," I said. "I'm going to draw a little more in the sketchbook, then maybe you'll want to add some. You can be like... a guest artist. Once in a while. If you want. And if you won't go blabbing about it to everyone."

"Sure," said Bee, and she climbed back up into the tree while I sat on the ground with Vivi and worked on this section. I'm going to leave the sketchbook with Bee for tonight.

Goosy says life is a daring adventure* or nothing. I guess "nothing" would be pretty boring.

This is Bee!

Some people are scared to be up in the air, but not me.

My name is Abby. Bee for short! I'm 11. I like to climb trees.

I like to climb high, where I can look down and watch what everyone else is doing

ONE DAY...

I was climbing my favorite tree near the park, and I found this notebook with drawings in it!

It was Aldo's!

I recognized him from my baseball team. I thought his sketchbook was a great idea,

so I decided to draw in it too.

It was fun to watch Aldo and Jack as they looked for me.

I was there at the swimming pool.

That's me with the rub-on tattoo

I was the girl climbing the tree when they were riding their bikes with Slushies. I was even up in the fort tree on the day Aldo got his black eye and he went to the fort to write about it.

I don't have an artsy grandma like Goosy, but I do like to draw.

What else do I like? I like to run. I like to try new things. I like vegetables.

I have a sister named Genevieve. She's four. I have two cats—Ping and Pong.

And now I have two new friends— Aldo and Jack!

(At least I hope so.)

LUNCHBOX CLUB

Here we are in the fort—me and Jack and Bee. I told her she could meet us here today IF she brought snacks. She brought homemade chocolate chip cookies. Nice touch.

She also brought an old chair cushion, a cooler we can keep stuff in, and a pocket knife.

"Every fort should have a pocket knife," she said, and I had to agree.

"This fort has plenty of room for three," said Jack affably.*

"I guess so," I said.

Then Jack and I thumb-wrestled while Bee climbed to the top of the tree.

She wanted to tack one of her flower drawings to the trunk of the tree, but I had to put my foot down there. NO MORE FLOWERS. Not in the fort, and not in the sketchbook.

You know what's amazing? This sketchbook is almost full! I'm going to put it back in the lunchbox for now and have Bee tuck it up in the tree, so that:

1. no more girls will find it, and

2. it'll be safe and sound till I return.

Maybe Goosy will buy me another sketchbook if I finish this one. I think I'd like to start a second one. What should I draw next?

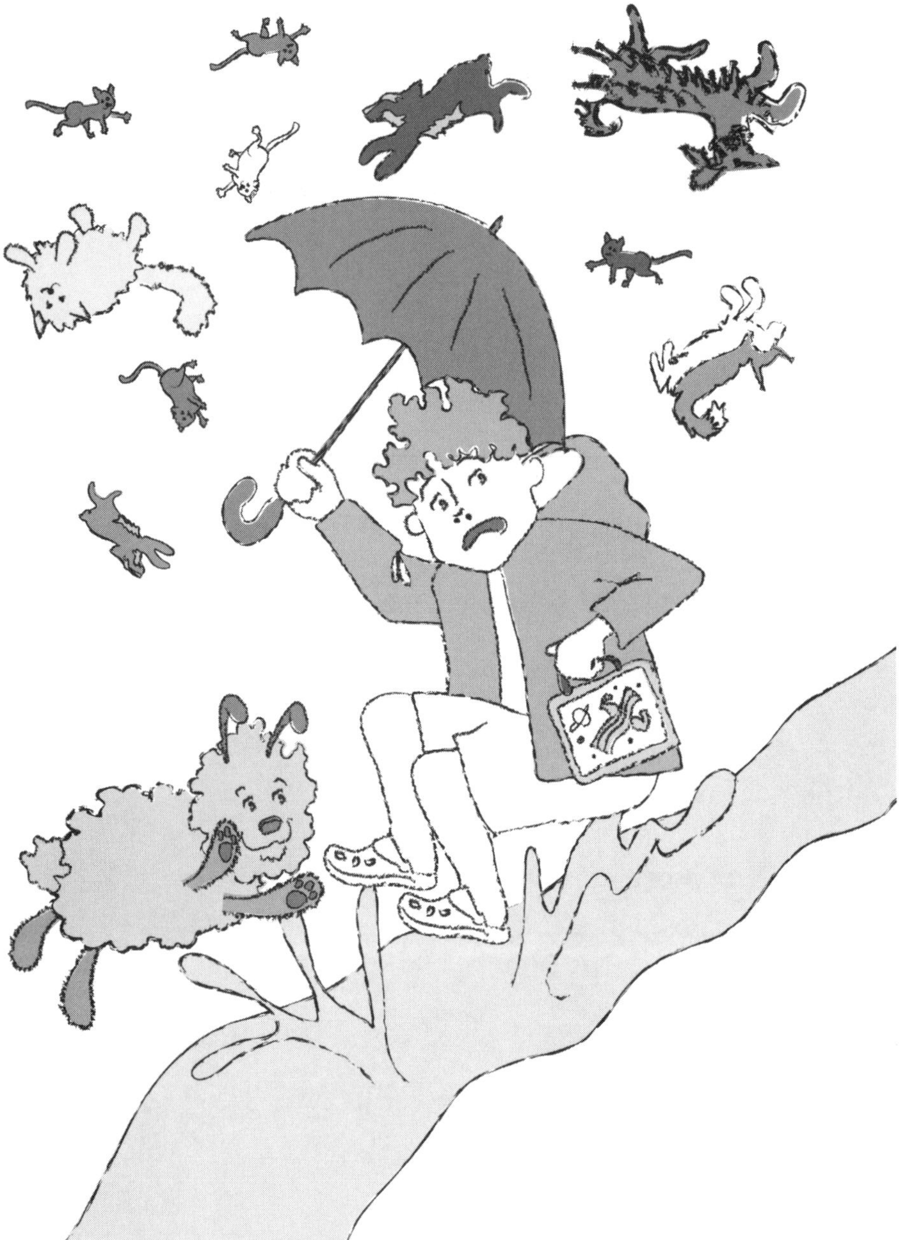

ARTSY-FARTSY

It rained today. Baseball got cancelled for me and Timothy, and so did Mom's bird group outing. Dad invited Goosy and Mr. Mot over for homemade pizza. He said it was an oven-warming kind of June day.

I put on my raincoat to get the lunchbox from the fort. It's too wet to draw outside, but it's a good day to draw inside.

When you live where it doesn't rain very much, like I do, it's easy to forget that jumping in puddles is one of the very best things about summer. Even I like to go OUTSIDE and get sopping wet in a downpour. (Sweaty is bad wet. Rainy is good wet.)

I had fun stomping down to the fort in the rain, but on the way back, it really started raining cats and dogs. And it thundered super loud. That freaked me out, so Max and I ran home as fast as we could, back home where it's toasty-warm and dry and smells like the next best thing to chicken enchiladas.

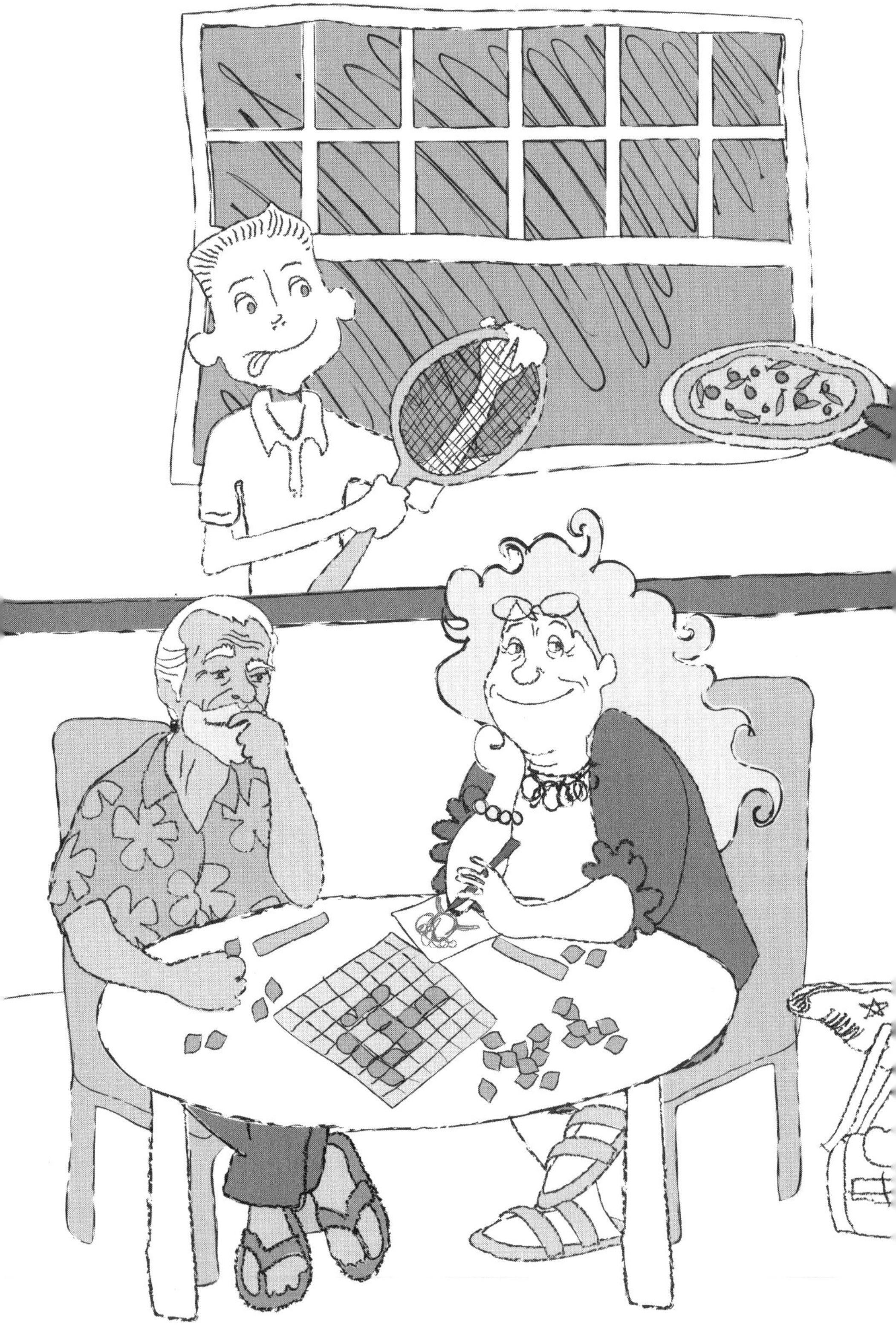

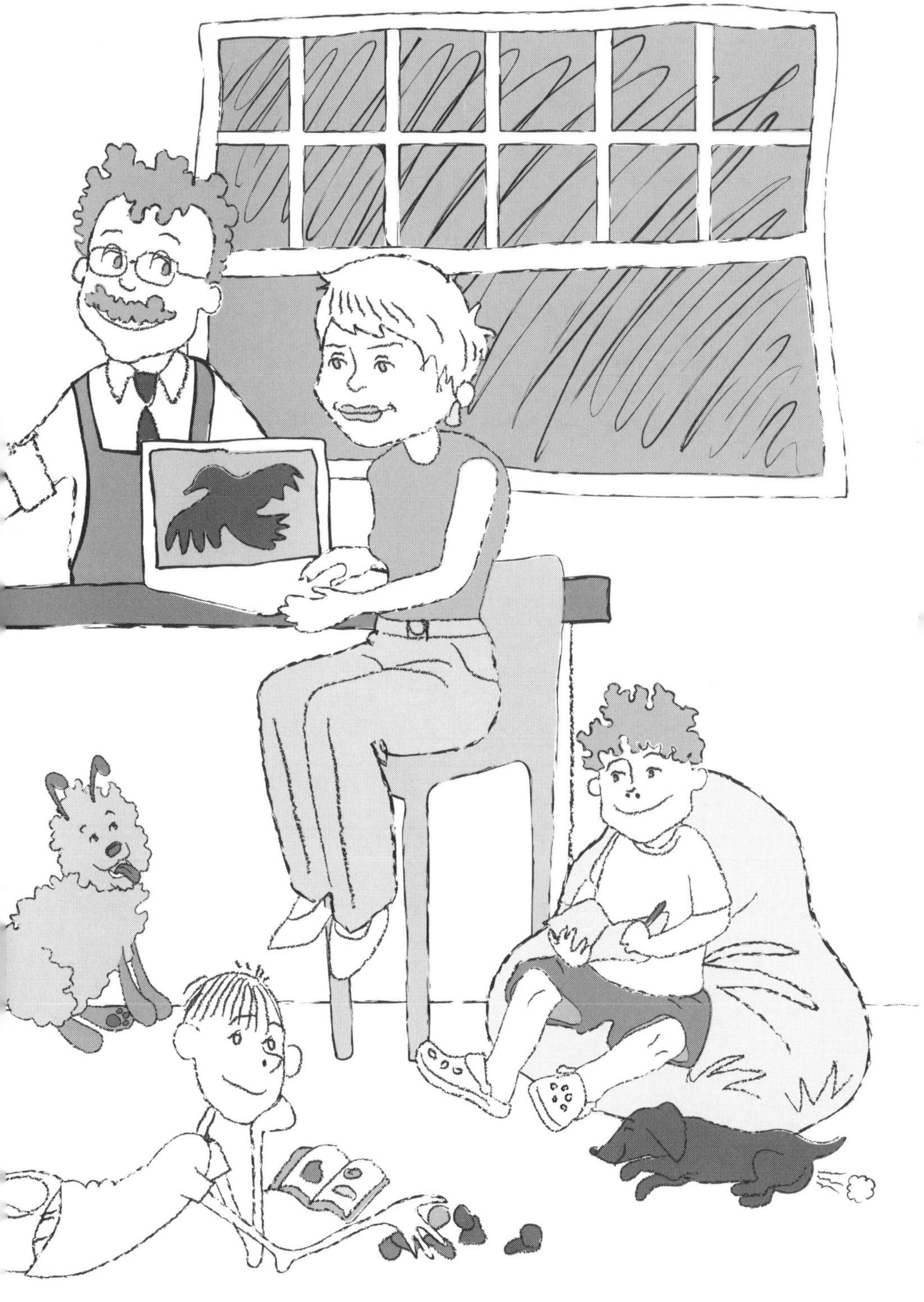

So here I am, sitting here in my favorite chair. (Yeah it's made out of beans. So what?) I'm looking around the room and noticing that all my favorite people are doing their favorite things.

Everyone is doing something different, yet we're together. And, we're all doing things we like to do—things that give us that buzzing-with-aliveness feeling.

Even Slate, who is tooting (I know, because now I can smell that, too) seems to be enjoying himself.

So I guess that's what it means to be artsy-fartsy. Seems like everyone is artsy-fartsy, each in our own way. Even Tommy Geller.

I'm going to finish this page then show the sketchbook to Mr. Mot and Goosy. I think they'd like to see it again now that it's full.

Bye for now. I mean adios. Au revoir. Arrivederci. Auf wiedersehen. Aloha. *Annyonghi gaseyo!*

How to say goodbye
in six different languages:

Adios	Spanish
Au revoir	French
Arrivederci	Italian
Auf wiedersehen	German
Aloha	Hawaiian
Annyonghi gaseyo	Korean

MY NEIGHBORHOOD

BASEBALL FIELD

BEE'S HOUSE

BEE'S CLIMBING TREE

MY HOUSE

MR. MOT' HOUSE

SWIMMING POOL

SQUIRREL GIRL'S HOUSE

GOOSY'S HOUSE

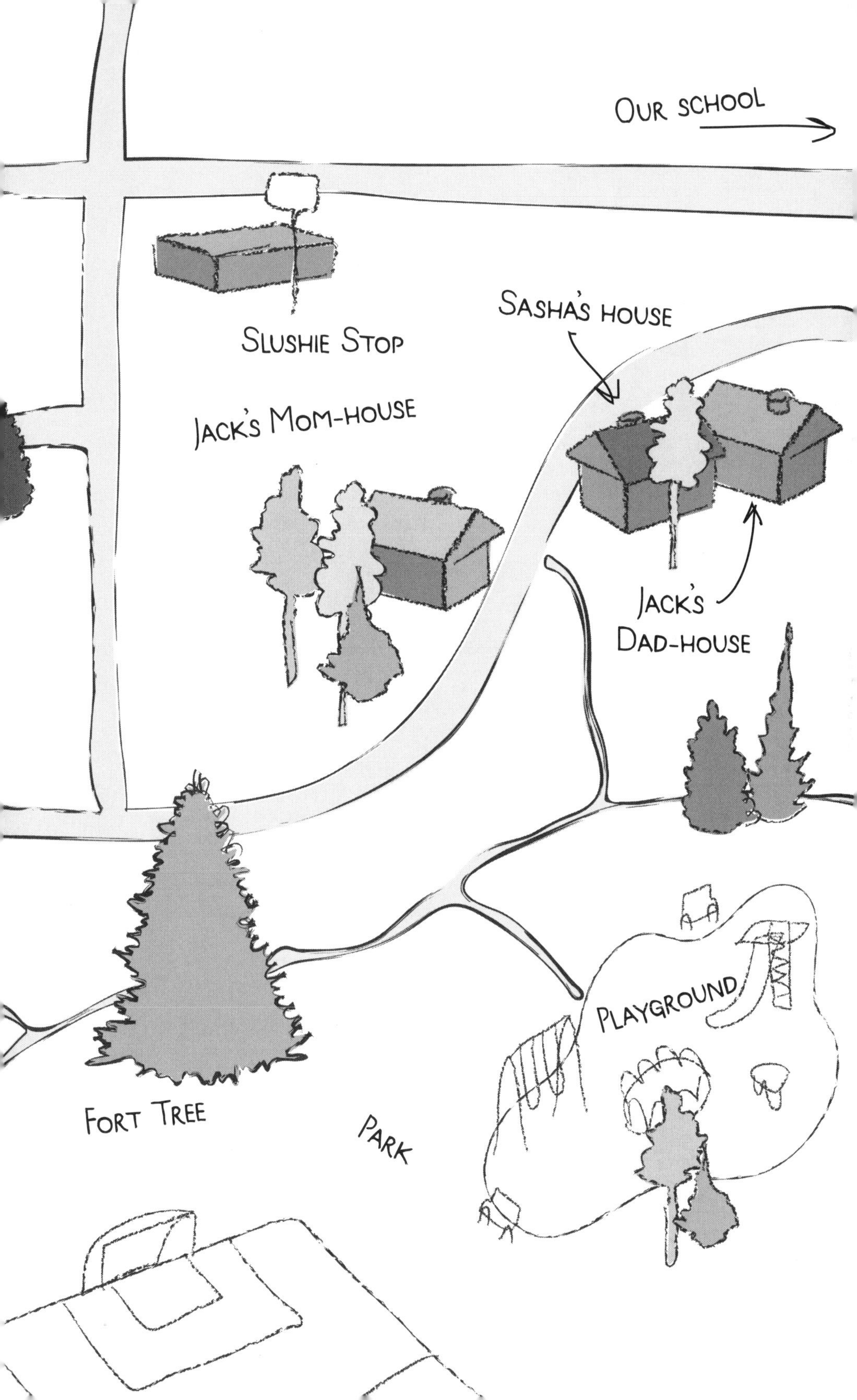
OUR SCHOOL
SLUSHIE STOP
SASHA'S HOUSE
JACK'S MOM-HOUSE
JACK'S
DAD-HOUSE
PLAYGROUND
FORT TREE
PARK

"A" GALLERY

When I first got this sketchbook and I didn't know what to draw or write, Mr. Mot told me I should start at the very beginning.

Then he marked a couple of cool A words I'd written with one of these things * (which is called—I just now realized he was trying to be funny—an asterisk. Get it? Word nerd humor.). So as I was working on the book, he suggested other rock-candy A words, and I popped them in here and there. I asterisked them all. If you don't know what some of them mean, you can look here, in the Gallery. If you don't know how to say some of them, just ask Mr. Mot. Or someone you know who's like Mr. Mot. Or go to aldozelnick.com, and we'll say them for you.

aardvark: some weird little animal that eats ants. But you know what's cooler? An aardwolf! For real! It's a stripy hyena-like guy with big ears that eats termites.

ABC gum: It's Already Been Chewed.

abominable: something that's so awful and bad that you need a fancy five-syllable word to say how awful it is

absurd: something that seems like it's too ridiculous to be true (but just might be true anyway)

abut: when two things join up right next to each other. Colorado abuts Nebraska. My back abuts my butt. (My mom says that's not appropriate.*)

abysmal: really, really, hopelessly bad (the abyss of badness)

accidentally on purpose: pretending something was an accident when really it was completely and totally on purpose

acronym: when you call something by its initials, like M.G. (Did you know that the word "scuba" is an acronym? It stands for <u>s</u>elf-<u>c</u>ontained <u>u</u>nderwater <u>b</u>reathing <u>a</u>pparatus.)

acrophobic: afraid to be in high places [Not me!]

addled: confused and mixed up

ad nauseum: over and over and over and over and over and over and over and over and over and over again, until you're so tired of it you want to throw up

adventure: something you do that's thrilling, even if you don't know for sure that it's going to have a good ending

affably: nicely, amiably*

aficionado: people who like something so much that they spend a lot of time and energy doing it and learning about it. For example, Jack is definitely a rock aficionado.

agape: wide open

agate: a kind of rock made of quartz, which is also a kind of rock, so...yeah

agitation: being anxious and annoyed, together

ajar: open just a little bit

A.K.A.: also known as

alert: I don't know... what's a lert? Do you have a lert in your house? (Just kidding. It means paying close attention to what's going on around you.)

alien: a being from outer space OR just somebody who's in a place where he or she doesn't belong, like me on a running track

allergic: when your body says, "whoa, that stuff is really uncool" and gets all red and puffy to show its annoyedness

alliteration: when you use a few words in a row that have the same starting sound, like... Jack jumped juice jars. (Jack says that's dumb.)

alluring: smells or looks so good that you want to get closer to it, like just-baked chocolate cake on the counter

amalgam: different things mixed together

ambidextrous: able to do things with either your right hand or your left hand

ambitious: challenging

ambivalent: when you feel both good and bad about something at the same time

ambled: walked slowly, as if you didn't care

ambrosial: I have no idea.

149

America's pastime: our country's nickname for baseball. It means we love it so much it's like our national sport. Which is absurd.

amiable: friendly, easy-going

amiss: not normal or right. For example:

A SWING AND A MISS!

amuck: wildly, out of control

anagram: when you scramble up the letters of a word and make other words out of the same letters. How many different words can you make of the letters S-T-R-E-A?

ancient: 50 years old or older

angelic: perfect, like an angel, like... me!

annihilate: completely destroy

annoyed: a little mad and a little frustrated mixed together

anonymous: done by someone who didn't give her name or doesn't want us to know who she is

Antarctica: that continent on the bottom of the earth where penguins live

antidisestablishmen-tarianism: A real word! Count how many letters. No clue what it means, but it's impressive.

apoplectic: crazy, excited, red-in-the-face mad

appalling: same as abominable, only not quite as bad because it's only three syllables

apprehensive: kind of scared about something you think is going to happen, like when you're in the waiting room at the doctor's office and you think you're going to get a shot

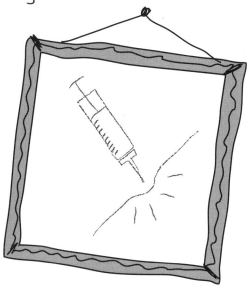

appropriate: people think it's OK to do

approximately: about

apt: fitting, accurate

aptitude: what you're naturally good at

arbitrary: random

archenemy: your very worst enemy

artsy-fartsy: artistic, creative. Sometimes when people call someone artsy-fartsy, they mean he or she is trying to show off by being artistic. But Goosy told me she thinks artsy-fartsy just means being creative and having fun with it.

asinine: super, mega, ultra, über dumb

askance: when you look at someone sideways, out of the corner of your eyes and frown because you don't trust or believe the person.

askew: crooked, tipped sideways

asparagus: a long, skinny green vegetable that no one likes. [Bee likes it!]

assume: when you believe something is true even though you don't have good evidence that it is

astonishing: so amazing that when you see it or hear about it, your mouth goes agape

athletic: coordinated, fast, strong, good at sports and moving your body. So what.

attitude: how you express the feelings you have inside about something

auburn: Mr. Mot says that Squirrel Girl's hair isn't reddish-brown...it's auburn (which means reddish-brown! hello!).

audacious: something that's very cool and also kind of brave

augment: add onto, make bigger, increase

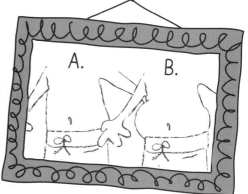

authority: leaderishness

authorize: using your leaderishness to say that something is OK

awkward: weird and uncomfortable-feeling

Visit **aldozelnick.com** to…

- learn more about the next book
  in the series.

- hear how to pronounce the
  Gallery words.

- get Mr. Zelnick's snickerdoodle recipe.

- download coloring pages.

- see Karla and Kendra's appearance
  schedule or invite them to your school,
  bookstore, or event.

- sign up for our e-mail list.

Hey, everybody,
I'm tweeting!
Follow me on Twitter:
@AldoZelnick

PUBLISHED JULY 2010

PUBLISHED MAY 2011

Ten-year-old Aldo Zelnick had decided it's OK to be a *little* artsy-fartsy. So when his grandma Goosy gives Aldo a second sketchbook, he fills it with more hand-drawn comics, rock-candy B words, and accounts of his everyday adventures.

Aldo and his best friend, Jack, find a ring in the storm grate on their street. Convinced it's fake, Aldo goofs around with the ring and loses it—only to find out it was a *real* diamond with a $1,000 reward!

Will Aldo, Jack, and Bee find the ring again and reap the reward...or will their archenemy, Tommy Geller?

And what would Aldo do with $1,000, anyway?

For readers 7-13 | 160 pages | Hardcover
ISBN 978-1-934649-06-0 | $12.95

Summer is drawing to a close, and the Zelnicks travel to the family farm in Minnesota for their vacation. Aldo's mom is eager for him to experience the things she loved as a girl...shucking sweet corn, milking cows, gathering eggs. A week of FRESH AIR and living off the land!

But Aldo suspects that farm life isn't all it's cracked up to be...and it's worse than he feared. The rooster wakes him at dawn, the chores nearly do him in, and Timothy and the cousins—identical twin pranksters—are in cahoots against him. Plus, the creepy, old portrait of his great-grandfather Aldo (the very one he's named after) seems to be watching him from his frame on the wall...

All this without the comforts of TV or computer—because the Anderson farm is (gasp!) technology-free.

For readers 7-13 | 160 pages | Hardcover
ISBN 978-1-934649-08-4 | $12.95

BAILIWICK PRESS

309 East Mulberry Street | Fort Collins, Colorado 80524 | (970) 672-4878
www.bailiwickpress.com | www.aldozelnick.com

ACKNOWLEDGMENTS

"We should all do what, in the long run,
gives us joy, even if it is only
picking grapes or sorting the laundry."
— E.B. White

This is a book about learning to revel in your own artsy-fartsyness, whatever it may be.

Words have always been my thing. Maybe it's because as a toddler I was introduced to Scrabble on my mother's lap, or maybe it's because I learned early the pleasure of escaping into a good book.

Kendra was artsy-fartsy before she ever realized it. She's grateful to have parents who have always encouraged her to try new things. Some stick, some don't. But there's always curiosity and there's always creativity—in building an ontological argument, cobbling together a phrase in Russian, improvising in the kitchen, or monkeying around with a bike.

But enough about us. This page is supposed to be about *you*.

We thank everyone who helped us, inspired us, and cheered us on.

I've been in the Slow Sand Writers Society since it was founded in 1994. Its members, past and present, are among my dearest friends and most patient, unstinting supporters. They midwifed this book. Leslie Patterson and Teresa Funke counted its fingers and toes.

My kids—Seth, Andy, and especially Eli—inspired this story, its characters, and its form. My husband, Scott, said *go for it* and picked up the slack at home so I could.

Designer Launie Parry made the cover a work of art in and of itself.

Thanks to Kendra's family for overlooking her habit of drawing at the dinner table, even after it stopped being crayons and started being a laptop. Her sister and right hand, Dana, cooked for her more nights than not, and rewarded milestones with projects, baked goods, and outings. Kendra also appreciates every one of you who got sick of hearing her say "I can't—I gotta work" but stayed supportive and kept the invites coming anyway.

Kid draft readers Talia Berlin, AJ Buckner, Braden Wormus, Victor Amato, Ava Funke, Lydia Funke, Katie Parry, Andy Oceanak, and Eli Oceanak told us what was working and, more important, what wasn't.

And finally, without our Aldo Angels, this book simply would not exist. Crucial and astonishingly generous financial support aside, they provided us with something even more essential: an oh-geez-we-really-have-to-finish-this-because-we-promised-it deadline. We're agog with gratitude. (If you're on the list on the following page: A is for abscond. We seriously discussed taking your money and blowing it on a trip to Paris. But instead we stayed home, and what do you know? Turns out you sent us on our way, after all.)

Karla Oceanak
October, 2009

ALDO'S ANGELS

Do you believe in us? we asked.

Where do we send the check? they answered, without a moment's hesitation.

We've been flabbergasted and deeply touched by their support, and we dedicate this book to them, our Aldo Angels.

Barbara Anderson

Meg Anderson

Carol & Wes Baker

Cindy Bergum

Butch Byram

Susie Cannon

Anne Conklin

Annie Dahlquist

Mike & Pam Dobrowski

Laurie Engeldinger

Leigh Waller Fitschen

Teresa Funke

Chris Goold

Sawyer Gray (and Chris & Sarah)

Griff Griffin

Alesia Gural

Thomas & Nancy Hadam

Calvin Halvorson & Bennett Zent (and Chet)

Maggie Hayes

Dick & Peggy Hohm

Chris Hutchinson

IBPAB (Jana Knezovich, Kathy Kosec, Linda Mahan, Starr Teague & Jacki Witlen)

Vicki & Bill Krug

Josh Lehman

Clint & Stacey Lucas

Annette Lynch

Virginia MacKinnon

Reid, Megan & Gwyneth Maulsby

Matt Messinger

Jody & Greg Motz

Kristin Mouton

Marge Norskog

Jackie O'Hara

Betty Oceanak

Craig Oceanak

Alveta Petersen

Jackie Peterson

Ryan Petros

Erin Poynter & Matthew Harrison

Erin Rogers

Terri Rosen

Roberta Satterfield

John Schiller & Suzanne Holm

Patty & Ray Seaser

Gregory Shannon

Slow Sand Writers Society

Barb & Steve Spanjer

Dana Spanjer

Jeanie Sutter

Sandy Thomson

Vince & Adrianne Tranchitella

Lynn Utzman-Nichols

ABOUT THE AUTHOR

Karla Oceanak has been a voracious reader her whole life and a writer and editor for more than twenty years. In her career as a marketeer, Karla has written everything you can imagine, from brochures and packaging copy to ads, video scripts, and feature articles. She has also ghostwritten numerous self-help books. She lives with her husband, Scott, and their three boys in a house strewn with Legos, hockey gear, Pokémon cards, video games, books, and dirty socks in Fort Collins, Colorado. This is her first novel.

ABOUT THE ILLUSTRATOR

Kendra Spanjer divides her time between being "a writer who illustrates" and "an illustrator who writes"— an ambitious amalgam, indeed. She decided to cultivate her artistic side after discovering that the best part of chemistry class was entertaining her peers (and her professor) with "The Daily Chem Book" comic. Since then, her diverse body of work has appeared in a number of group and solo art shows, book covers, marketing materials, fundraising events, and public places. When she invents spare time for herself to fill, Kendra enjoys skiing, cycling, exploring, discovering new music, watching trains go by, decorating cakes with her sister, and making faces in the mirror.